The Primrose

Patience H. Jacoby

National Library of Canada Cataloguing in Publication Data

Jacoby, Patience H., 1967-
The primrose

ISBN 1-55369-114-8

I. Title.

PR6110.A36P7 2002 823'.92 C2001-904018-0

TRAFFORD

This book was published *on-demand* in cooperation with Trafford Publishing.
On-demand publishing is a unique process and service of making a book available for retail sale to the public taking advantage of on-demand manufacturing and Internet marketing. **On-demand publishing** includes promotions, retail sales, manufacturing, order fulfilment, accounting and collecting royalties on behalf of the author.

Suite 6E, 2333 Government St., Victoria, B.C. V8T 4P4, CANADA

Phone	250-383-6864	Toll-free	1-888-232-4444 (Canada & US)
Fax	250-383-6804	E-mail	sales@trafford.com
Website	www.trafford.com		

TRAFFORD PUBLISHING IS A DIVISION OF TRAFFORD HOLDINGS LTD.

Trafford Catalogue #01-0516 www.trafford.com/robots/01-0516.html

10 9 8 7 6 5 4 3 2

For my wonderful Thomas –
Without you, this story would never have been.

Denise –
You would have been so proud!

CHAPTER 1

A knock on the door tore him from the arms of the Lady Sleep. She had granted him comfort and sweet memories that night, and it took Tom a few moments to remember where he was. It all came flooding back. He jumped up with the enthusiasm and spirit of young love. His dreams were forgotten that very instant. This was Friday, the day his adventure really started!

A second knock focused his thoughts on the door. His senses came together and rushed him into the present – room service was to wake him at 4:45 with a Scottish breakfast. He picked up the hotel's bathrobe and went to let the waiter in. A boy who looked too young to be working this early in the morning carried a massive tray from which there emanated a multitude of delicious aromas. Even at a quarter to five on a Friday morning, this morning's feast aroused his appetite.

After a quick visit to the bathroom, he sat at the table and lifted the lids off the various plates. Theres had thought of everything. There was freshly squeezed orange juice, hot and strong coffee, and then the delights of the local cuisine: rich and creamy porridge (of the sweet variety, he hoped), cooked tomatoes and mushrooms, and a plate-full of different types of meat and sausages. Theres had called it a 'hearty breakfast', and that it was. He would not dare to not try a bit of everything, as he was sure she had her spies even in the kitchens of the hotel.

Theres – the name stirred pictures and emotions and so much more than anybody else before. Much more than he had imagined when he first found her as an Internet pen pal only a few months ago. Her invitation to write to her had interested him, and within days he had been hooked. Her intellect had fascinated him, her depth had at times perplexed him, her honesty had unsettled him more than once, and her beauty he simply admired. Within a couple of weeks, they had covered more ground and had got to know each other better than he had ever known anybody before. The journey they had traveled had been exhilarating and at times frightening. The journey ahead of them would be the culmination, and he had high hopes and expectations.

When she had suggested this time together, he had been more than willing to oblige her every whim. Initially this meant agreement on a budget for the next few weeks, which he was sure she would not meet, and the rest he had to leave with her alone. She had sent him a list of items to pack – and a list of items that he was sure not to pack. She sent him his plane tickets that had brought him to Aberdeen, where she had met him at the airport on Wednesday late afternoon. She had taken him to the hotel where they had had dinner and where she told him what to do on Thursday and how to prepare himself for Friday – when their journey together would start. She still had some work to do till then, some 'loose ends to tie up'. She had left him with a few tourist brochures introducing him to town, and when he later looked at them, he found a whole set of notes she had scribbled into the margins, highlighting the parts of exhibitions and architecture that she wanted him to see and appreciate. She was right of course – he had asked to see things her way and she had made sure he would.

During the dinner on Wednesday, he had given her the keepsake he had brought for her. He knew she was not wearing a lot of jewelry, but he had come across a tender little pendant that held a pressed flower. A pressed and thus preserved primrose. He had given this to her, casually commenting on the significance of the petals. Theres had thought for a while, and then smiled and nodded.

'You mean the primrose path of dalliance, don't you? I have read Hamlet and seen it several times. Shakespeare used a lot of symbolism like that in his work. And you know I like Hamlet.'

She sat there and looked at him and he could almost see her thoughts form behind her soft forehead.

'Are you trying to tell me something?'

Tom felt slightly embarrassed and uncomfortable. Of course he had known that she would understand the true meaning of his small present. She sat and watched his unease without coming to his aid.

'Aren't you going to help me put this on?' she had eventually asked.

Tom felt relieved that Theres had not objected to his choice, as they both were clear over his doubts about the future of their relationship. Both of them had their lives, their responsibilities, and they both had to accept this as fact.

Apart from the dinner on Wednesday and a hurried lunch on Thursday, he had not seen her. They had spoken briefly on the phone the previous night when she checked up on him being back in time from his sojourns into town for an early night. She was in control and Tom was beginning to wonder whether this was a good thing or a bad thing, and he realized that he trusted she would make sure he would love every minute of their journey.

The message for the day had been 'make sure to have a hearty breakfast (booked it for 4:45) and meet you in reception at 5:45 – we have a train to catch, so don't be late. PS: comfortable clothes but make sure you have your posh suit ready'. Yes, the posh suit. She had emailed him to inquire whether he had a dark ('blue or gray would do') three-piece suit, 'one with a waistcoat'. He had wondered what she wanted with that, before finding the piece at the back of his wardrobe. If Theres asked for a three-piece suit, he would make sure to take one.

After breakfast, he went back to the bathroom and turned on the shower. He wanted to be fresh and clean for her. This early in the morning, the water was hot and plentiful, something not to be taken for granted in a Scottish hotel. With his stomach now happily filled, Tom was at ease with his excitement. He knew he would appreciate every little morsel of what she had prepared for him. He also knew that he would simply have to get to know her better and more intimately over the next two or so weeks. It was his ultimate goal and one he would enjoy achieving.

He slung a towel round his waist and quickly wiped the steam off the mirror. His own face looked back at him. Tom stared.

What was he doing here? In only another three years, he would reach 60. It didn't show on his face as yet, but it was only a question of time and a few late nights, before his age would catch up with his body. He was frightfully aware of this. He also carried too much girth. Theres said neither mattered. She said that she loved the way he made her feel, and yet he worried that he might not be able to keep up with her. Theres, his beautiful companion for an exciting journey into the unknown. A journey to wherever it pleased her. He so wanted to please her. But when he looked at his face closely, he wondered whether he would be able to.

Almost mechanically, he shaved. No matter what his anxieties were, it simply would not do to let her wait. He was on a schedule, dictated by her, and he would do his utmost to keep to it. There was no going back now.

CHAPTER 2

When he got to reception, she was already there, checking out for him. He knew she traveled light, but was surprised when he saw not only a holdall but also a rather large suitcase on wheels and a backpack that seemed to be quite heavy. When he took a closer look at the woman herself, he noticed the infamous dungarees she was wearing as well as the hiking boots that had been with her even through her wedding day. He could make out the faint glimmer of the silver chain that held the little primrose petals around her neck. He wondered whether she had brought the dark red silk dress she had mentioned, floor length and made for her, enhancing the wonderfully gentle curves he expected lay under the ready-for-anything exterior.

Theres saw him coming, nodded at him briefly and said, 'Right on time, good'. Then she signed the credit card slip the receptionist had pushed her way. When she turned to face him, she smiled at him (O, how he could lose himself in that smile!) and asked: 'Ready?'

Tom thought for a second, before he replied.

'Sure am, just don't know what for.'

This earned him another of those smiles. She had warned him about this smile. She was well aware of what she could do to a man by just smiling 'that smile' and now Tom believed her.

She put away her wallet and grabbed her various pieces of luggage.

'Can I help you carry something?' Tom ventured but she shook her head.

'The moment I can't carry my own stuff I start traveling light'.

With that she pushed her way through the exit doors, leading him across the road outside into the railway station. There, she moved quickly on to the platform furthest away, where a train already stood waiting.

At the gate, a ticket collector asked for their tickets and she took a few moments to collect them from one of the many pockets on her dungarees. Once through the barriers, she spotted their carriage and with the experience of the frequent traveler, shifted all her gear onto the corridor of the train before boarding herself. Tom had barely time to follow before Theres had located their seats, deposited her case and holdall in the luggage compartment and thrown her rucksack onto one of the seats. Only then did she turn to him and help him along with his own baggage. Tom noticed that she seemed in a rush. When he inquired about this, Theres once again smiled.

'I want this to be just perfect, and I am glad you play along. I promise you, you will love this,' she said, pushed him onto a seat and placed herself opposite.

They were in a first-class compartment, and all by themselves. As if she could read his thoughts (and he almost believed she could), Theres offered 'I thought it would be nice travelling just by ourselves, just this bit of the journey.'

'Are you going to tell me where we are going?'

'Well, you told me that you liked the travel much more than the arrival, so we are going to be on the move for a while. But don't fret, this is not going to be stressful – as long as you sit back and let me do as I wish. It's all planned and you are here to enjoy.'

Tom smiled. His eyes drank in her youth that, at times, shone through more than it should. Sometimes, he thought he was with a teenager, impatient and aggressive; and, at other times, the woman opposite him was so much older than her years. Once again he became conscious that he had to be very careful not to completely and utterly fall for this enigmatic creature that had taken over his life so irrevocably.

She continued, oblivious (and maybe just on a schedule) of his feelings:

'You also said that you wanted to experience things that I like, and to see things the way I do. You asked me about my 'placeness', and this is the first part of it. This is a journey that I have made many times before, so I have been able to plan this to the last detail. I know there are so many things that you want to talk about and do, but please be patient and wait.' She glanced at her watch. 'The next three hours and ten minutes are my present to you.'

Tom was speechless. Just when he thought he knew what to say, the train started to move away from the platform, and Theres stood up. She lifted her rucksack onto the table that separated them, and undid some buckles. She rummaged around before taking out a small black box, which had a set of headphones wrapped around them.

'Now, my love – you asked for the complete package, and this is what you are going to get. This is my mp3 player, and I want you to listen to some music while you are looking out the window.'

She unwound the headphones and held them out for him. Her eyes beckoned him and even though he was not really in the mood for her play, he took them. He wanted to talk to her, wanted to find out about her and share his feelings, but how could he deny these eyes?

She sat again, opposite him, and he hooked the headphones into his ears. Theres was, he noticed, still in control of the little black box. He couldn't hear at first, and just when he was about to tell her that there was no sound, he made out the faint whine of a cello. The music gently grew louder and he turned his gaze to the view outside.

The sun rose creamy gray over an angry horizon. Clouds hung heavy and threatening in its path. It was late August, but the wind had been blowing quite strong and cold through town; but here, so close to the water's edge, Tom realized that there must have been a gale blowing over the North Sea. White foam spewed around a sad, sandy beach. The train was going along the coast, on a track that was some hundred feet above the ocean, right along a craggy cliff edge. Only a few feet of grass separated the track from the depth. He wondered whether any trains ever had been blown over. The music in his ears moved in time with the scenery. Even though the world outside seemed unfriendly and cold, combined with Pachelbel's Canon for string quartet, Tom felt at home inside. And suddenly he understood Theres just a little bit more.

After Montrose and its strange in-land harbor, the landscape changed. With the new views outside, Theres had changed the music. There suddenly were pipes, and the driving beat of an electric guitar. He had never experienced music like this, and had only dreamt of such scenery only a few feet away. If he had been worried about the closeness of the abyss before, he now felt the thrill and excitement of a child on a fast and frantic merry-go-round. The train had picked up speed and the track was ever closer to the edge of the cliffs. There was no green strip, there was nothing but craggy cliffs and the ever-angry waters of the North Sea. His face moved closer to the window, till in the end, his nose was almost pressed against it, his hand fighting, reaching out to grasp on the images flying past outside. The music reached a crescendo as the waves pounded against the shore. And then, suddenly, Theres turned off the music and the train drew into Dundee.

'That was … fantastic', was all he could say. The journey had lasted no more than an hour, but he was hooked.

'You know, this bit of the journey is the best I have ever come across. The rest of the way is … well … just to get there. Nothing special. And we have to change in Edinburgh. Did you really like it?' There was a hint of insecurity in her voice now.

'Dearest, if you weren't that far away, I would kiss you right now!'

When she moved across to sit beside him, Tom pulled her close, kissed and kissed her again.

'And I like your choice of music. What was that second piece I was listening to?'

'That was one of my all-time favorite pieces by a local band. Liked it?'

Tom nodded, still holding her close to him.

'It's called 'ghillies'. It's wonderful, don't you think? One day, I want to write the choreography to this. I can see it in my head already; dozens of dancers swirling round and round, with all the changes in the beat ...'

In reply, he kissed her again. The train moved on and they sat in silence, holding on to each other, till Edinburgh.

From there, it was barely six hours on the fast train to London's Victoria Station. They had seats beside each other and the time flew with chat and deep conversation, and both found each other titillating and captivating travel companions. The ice was broken, there was no need any longer to hold back any thoughts. At the same time, Tom's trust in her capabilities and organizational skill let him believe that Theres could do anything she set her mind to. Getting him there, onto the train with her, was just a small prelude to what this woman could and would do.

In London, by now tired from the journey and the early start to the day, Theres knew her way. She put the entire luggage into storage, found them a seat at a café, and outlined his orders for the next two hours.

'I have to leave you, but we need to meet at the place where we dropped off the luggage in two hours exactly. Eight o'clock that is. Don't forget. There are shops along there,' she pointed, 'but don't buy anything – it is extremely expensive here. Out there,' she pointed in another direction 'is where you can have a shower and if you like, get changed. But you don't have to – yet. Just meet me back at the luggage place in two hours.'

Before he could acknowledge having understood all she had said, she left, leaving him sitting there by himself.

Suddenly the promise of two whole hours without Theres seemed a sad prospect to Tom. He strolled along to the shops, and indeed found their merchandise extremely overpriced. He wondered where she had gone and hoped she would be back sooner rather than later; he missed her already. For a brief minute, he thought about his family back home and all the things they had said when he told them about his journey. They did not know about Theres and he wondered what they would say or do should they ever find out. What did he know about her anyway? Not a lot. But what he knew was enough to make him want to be with her, if only this once. People would call him mad and all sorts of other names, but he had had to come and be here with her. She had two months before starting her new job in Detroit, and she had said that there was nobody she would rather spend her time travelling with. How could he have disappointed her?

After an hour and a quarter, he found his way to their pre-arranged meeting point and sat down. He watched people go by, some happy, some sad, but all involved in travel. At least it seemed so. Travel was so fascinating, so liberating. There were people sweeping the floors, and there was a multitude of pigeons. The noise was unbearable at times, and he hardly ever could make out what was said over the tannoys.

Two hours were up and when he looked around, he could not see her. What if she had just left him there, stranded in London? All by himself? Fear and doubt overcame him. Suddenly, there was a hand on his shoulder.

Tom could not believe his eyes. She had said she 'scrubbed up nice', but this? She was beautiful. She had changed into a tight, nearly floor-length black and white skirt, and a coat that could have leapt out of the pages of a 1930's catalogue. It looked like cashmere and was down to her knees. There was a collar of astrakhan braid, and deep, large pockets. She wore a matching hat and, for the first time, make-up. His eyes melted into hers. He noticed her long lashes and the full, perfect lips now covered in a gentle rose-tinted lipstick. Theres leant over him and those same lips met his in a warm and tender embrace.

'Have you waited for me long?'

Tom had to force himself to answer, 'Didn't seem long at all.'

'Ready for the real surprise then?'

'Aren't you my surprise?'

'Och no', she growled in her fake Scottish accent. 'Come along now', took his hand and led him away.

There was a short queue and he could not make out where they were going. The platform they were bound for was set back from all the others and separated from the general hurly-burly of Victoria Station by a glass front. There was a sign, but Tom could not make out what it said, as people blocked his view. Theres held on to his hand; her warmth was flowing all over him, wrapping him in comfort and tenderness. A short way away, he could make out a black porter carrying their luggage. The man wore a uniform and above his polished brass buttons, his face smiled at him and Theres. The man nodded and winked, Theres smiled back, and then they were on the platform. A train stood waiting, a special train whose pictures Tom had seen more than once before, and which he immediately recognized. He should have known all along what was happening, that they were about to board the Orient Express!

Tom's heart beat faster. He had dreamt of this train and this journey so often, and now it was so close he could hardly believe it was happening.

Theres turned round to him, still holding on to his hand.

'Nice?'

'Very!'

Before he knew how it happened, they stood in a tight embrace. Time stood still as he could feel their bodies melting into each other. Theres lifted her face to look into his eyes and there was no turning back – ever. If later he would have to pinpoint the moment when he fell in love with her for real and for good, this would be it. Their lips met, with gentle pressure at first, but developed more intensity and heat as it went on.

'Let's go', she whispered and led him onto the train.

CHAPTER 3

The porter had already taken his case and bag into the compartment when the attendant opened the door for Tom and beckoned him to enter. The view and the prospect of spending the next day or so in these magnificent surroundings almost overwhelmed him. He found himself standing in the middle of a small, single room. The darkened window opposite the entrance door took in most of that side. He could watch the world outside without being watched himself. The paneling on his right and left was heavy, dark wood. On the left side, a settee was arranged with luscious velvet cushions, and a small table in the corner beneath the window was set with china, ready for tea to be poured. To his right were two doors. Tom turned and looked, committing every view to memory.

There was a short knock, and Tom looked around.

'Come in!'

One of the doors now opened and Theres stood in the doorway.

'Like it?'

'Where did you get to?' he asked, still taking it all in. Theres had taken off her coat and hat, and stood in her stockinged feet. She smiled, like a small child that expected praise for an excellent little achievement. His heart was beating faster. At this moment, he felt for her so intensely that he could hardly bear not to touch her then.

'I am in my room. You didn't think we were sharing, did you?' There was a mischievous twinkle in her eyes. She moved back through the doorway she had stood in, and his view opened to a small storage area where their luggage had been placed for them, and then farther on into her room, the mirror image of his. Her hat and coat she had thrown over the settee; her rucksack sat on the little dressing table, opened but waiting to be unpacked. Within seconds she had made the place hers, made this compartment in a strange train look like home.

'This is wonderful', Tom uttered, standing close to her and drinking in the scent of her tousled hair in front of him. 'How did you manage to get us onto this? I bet you blew the budget!'

Theres smiled and looked at him. 'Wouldn't you like to know? I just got chatting to the guy that takes the bookings, and while I was talking to him, someone cancelled this and I was first in line to jump in and got us this suite. Isn't this just wonderful? Aren't you impressed?'

Tom stretched out his arms and wrapped himself around her.

'I am impressed. It is wonderful. Just like a dream!' he whispered under his breath before his lips descended onto her wonderful warm and loving mouth. He just wanted to feel her lips with his, just for a short moment, but Theres responded in a way that he had imagined forever. Her mouth opened and her tongue pushed in between his lips, taking over and demanding all his attention. The kiss lingered and the passionate tension between their bodies became electric. When she pulled away, he felt disappointed.

'Have a look at the bathroom!' Her voice rang with excitement.

The second door from his room, like the other door in hers, led to their shared bathroom. The sink was set in a base of the same dark wood that paneled their rooms, taps shiny in gold, the toilet seat gleamed in white and a shower was taking possession of a suitable corner. A heap of towels was piled onto some shelves, and a selection of small glass bottles held the promise of luxuries they yet had to explore.

'There is going to be a Champagne reception later, so you better get dressed up. We don't want to be late, do we?'

She closed the connecting door. Tom was alone in the dark corridor that harbored their cases. He sighed and took hold of his suitcase, and then went back to his own cabin. He could not forget the taste of her lips and the feeling of her tongue in his mouth. He had wanted to continue, had wanted to pull her closer and keep her there, right there in his arms where he felt she belonged from hereon in. And there was so much more he wanted to do to her. He wanted to show her how much he loved her. He purely and simply wanted her.

A few minutes to ten, Theres knocked once again at his door. When she opened, she saw him tying his tie and running his comb through his hair. He was wearing his best suit, as he thought she would have appreciated. Another of those smiles honored him.

'I see you scrub up nice, too! Time to go, my love.'

She opened the door to the main corridor, waited for Tom to lock up and sink the key into his pocket. Then, she hooked her arm under his, and together they made their way to the restaurant car where Champagne and some of the other passengers waited.

They all raised their glasses, Tom could hear a faint whistle from outside, and the train began its journey. Sipping the fizziness that made his throat tingle, Tom smiled. There was no going back now, even if he had wanted to. All he could do was sit back and enjoy the future that Theres had planned for them.

A small party had developed, and she had wandered over to the pianist, no doubt entrancing him like all around her with her charm and wit. Tom felt proud when he saw the way other men looked at her. To think that she wanted to be with him was more than he ever had expected. He banished all thoughts of jealousy and concentrated on the joy her presence gave him.

Her hair caught the light and the blonde highlights made her head sparkle. She was an angel - his angel, and his desire for her rose again with every breath and every moment he spent in her presence. They had not met all that long ago, and he was not sure whether his passion for her was truly welcome or even reciprocated. There had been her kiss earlier, but that might have been the exuberance of her youth or the excitement of the starting journey. He would have to be careful not to frighten her away with his feelings, she was a treasure he intended to keep. The next day or so would bring them closer together, hopefully in more ways then one. Tom was almost certain of that.

After a while, the party dispersed. It was late and people went back to their own cabins. In a corner, some passengers played cards, but Theres looked tired and Tom offered to take her back to the suite. She walked in front of him and he could see the back of her lovely, lyre-shaped derriere move under the tight skirt. If only he knew her well enough to reach out and touch!

When they reached her door, she turned towards him.

'I think you should get yourself into something more comfortable, it is late', she said, and kissed him briefly, before leaving him. Just as she was closing the door, he caught her eye, saw a devilish glint, and excitement took over.

He entered his own room with gusto and tore at his clothes. Heat had entered his body like a flash of lightning, he felt young and keen and full of lust. His desire showed, his erection was hard and strong. Tom covered his body with nothing but his bathrobe. The settee had been turned into a bed in his absence, and he sat down. When he closed his eyes, all he could see was her. He imagined her body, pale and pure. His right hand moved to his erect penis, taking a good hold and gently massaging to ease the pressure that was rapidly accumulating in his balls. Theres ... he had often dreamt of her, before he ever knew she existed. The moment they had met on the Internet, his life had changed. There was no other for him, and he knew that he would have to be with her forever, one way or other. Life without her would be unbearable now that he had found her. His hand moved faster and faster as he imagined her generous, silken breasts rise with every breath she took. He imagined her nipples harden under his gaze, and stuck out his tongue like so many times before, just to pretend to butterfly over their pertness to see their response. Theres ...

The knock was so faint that it hardly reached his consciousness. He jumped up and his face turned bright red with embarrassment when he opened the door to an apparition of sensuality and beauty. Theres had changed into what seemed to be layers of gauze, wrapped around her like veils, see-through but only suggestive of her physical self beneath. Her hair was ruffled up and crowned her beautiful elfin face in the dim light that emanated from her room. She took in his embarrassment, but seemed to ignore the fainting evidence of his desire. When she stretched out her hand to reach for his, she said:

'Are you ready, my love? The evening has not ended yet! Come and see ...'

She led him into her room and he could see what she had arranged in the few minutes since she had been back. She must have been prepared, must have had it all planned out in her mind. The lights were dimmed, so that it felt like there were candles burning under the lampshades. Her bed was made up, like his, but she had put the cushions back and turned it into a lounger. The mp3 player from earlier had sprouted little loudspeakers and music rang quietly through the air. He did not recognize the tune, but it was some classical piece for violin. Theres had not only lowered the blinds, she had also drawn the heavy curtain. Tom found himself in the boudoir of his sensual angel.

He looked at her as she stood before him, wrapped in the dress that was nothing but layers of shiny voile, here and there catching the light and throwing flashes of sparkle back at him. Her nape was shiny and smooth; he could smell the delicate aroma of her perfect skin. He longed to sink his face in the small of her neck and drown in the moment. She stood there, feeling his eyes roam over her. She enjoyed the effect she had on him and allowed the instant to continue freely. Even though Tom had not been sure before of how far she would let him go, he stretched out his hand to touch the orb of her breast. He only wanted to touch gently, but she pushed him away so that he fell back onto the settee.

'Don't', she simply said. She turned, switched over the memory of her mp3 player and the music changed. This was modern, but still fairly quiet. By now he had come to value her sense of musical drama and he knew that she would have chosen something to underline her intentions for this evening. A delicious intensity rose within him and goose pimples ran over his body. He shivered. Theres motioned him to sit back further, and he pulled himself onto the settee full length, his back supported by the arm of the lounger. He made himself comfortable with a cushion beneath his shoulders, and he watched. His bathrobe had come undone and opened Theres' view of what he had to offer her. She gave away no approval but was focussed on what she had planned for him.

Theres stood in the middle of the room, and began to sway with the music. Her hips moved to and fro'; Tom gasped. He had held his breath but had to let go and grapple for air. She danced but not quite, she offered herself to him but didn't. She was his angel and his captor, and he knew that she was fully aware of what she was doing to him. He didn't care that she was playing, he was happy for now to be her toy.

The music picked up speed and Theres made the sign of the snake. As all dancers, she was extremely supple and she was also extremely proud of her own body and self, and she made the most of it. She turned him on, as was apparent by his reply to her movement. Theres' feet did not shift, her arms and upper body made all the moves. The fluency of her rhythm and the drama of her performance touched him deeply; the air was thick with eroticism and pure wantonness streamed from their bodies to mingle in the low lights as the train carried them south toward Paris.

When the first unknown and yet familiar song wormed its way to its crescendo, Theres turned about in time with the music, so that Tom could see her body moving past his eyes. He wanted her to slow down so that he could look at her fully and appreciate her even more, so he reached out. He only managed to get hold of her dress, but as Theres was still moving, he managed to pull the material off her shoulders. He gasped. In front of him, she stood naked.

Oblivious, Theres kept on dancing for him. The fragrance of oranges flowed from her shiny body. Tom noticed her silken skin and realized that she had clothed herself in scented oil. He looked on for another moment, and then he reached out and she stopped, right in front of him, so that he could hold on to her. His face sank onto her naked belly, his hair rubbing against her nakedness and picking up some of the oil she was wearing. Theres stood, her back stretched, her head tilted back and her eyes shut. As he touched her, a small moan escaped her lips. She shivered from his touch. The music played on, something exotic but quiet. The lovers were silent and motionless.

When he pulled her closer, she came willingly. She pushed the bathrobe off his shoulders - there was nothing he needed to hide any longer. Both were naked. Theres stretched towards the table and took hold of a small flask. She poured a little oil into her hands and then rubbed his back with the same scented oil that covered her body. Still no word. No words were needed.

Theres pulled him up and their arms took hold of each other. Their embrace was tight and for a while they just stood there, holding on to what they hoped never again to be without. Then, she kissed him. Her kiss was so much more, a confession of her love and evidence to him that she wanted to be with him as much as he with her. Gently, they swayed in time with the music. Tom's erection fitted nicely between her thighs. Her body's movement slowly stroked him and rubbed his glands. He could feel her creamy silken readiness leaching over him. Her breasts were pressed hard against his chest and Tom moved away a little to be able to finally touch her and see her nipples react. They did, just like in his dreams.

Theres' hands ran along his spine before settling around his neck. She pulled his head closer and then pushed it down so that his lips could meet her excited nipples. Tom gasped. He had dreamed of this so often, he had wanted to taste her so many times before, and now … now that it really happened, he wanted to take his time over it and give Theres - his Theres - as much of himself as she gave of herself.

'Suck me, please', Theres whispered.

When Tom sucked hard, careful not to actually hurt her, she meowed like a kitten.

'More', and he willingly obeyed her command. They moved gently and Tom maneuvered her closer to the bed. When the back of her knees touched it, Tom gently pushed against her, and they fell onto it. His weight pinned her below him. Their mouths were united in ever mounting passion. He touched her legs, she willingly opened. He found the dunes of her love strangely naked and the entry to her love free of any little hairs but oily and ready for him. He had never been with a woman that shaved her intimate places and he wondered whether it would make him feel different.

A long, single sigh rose from his throat as he pushed in. He was surprised to see the sparkle in her eyes when he looked down at her.

'I love you', he whispered.

'Love me some more', came her reply.

CHAPTER 4

The early morning sun found Tom in bed, alone. It took him a moment to realize that it was Theres' bed he was in, her things around him - her rucksack on the floor, her glasses on the little shelf by the window. He noticed the doors between their cabins open, and Theres stretched out in his own bed.

She was still asleep, her face relaxed and at peace. Her chest lifted and fell with each breath she took, the skin of her bare arms smooth above the sheets, the outline of her breasts covered by the thin material. Tom smiled as he remembered the previous night. He had made love to her like he hadn't made love in a very long time. She excited him, kept him going on and on and on, time and time again. She had been receptive of his every mood, and when she had wrapped her legs around his waist, not letting him go but sucking him deeper and deeper into her love, he forgot all else. He forgot that he was more than twenty years her senior, and could be her father. With her, time did not matter, and age was but a meaningless number. Their love was timeless and last night, it had become tangible.

Theres stirred. Before opening her eyes to the new day, she stretched like a cat, her arms above her head, her back arched, so that the blanket slipped off her upper body, her tantalizingly full breasts open for Tom to admire. When she turned, she smiled and stretched her hands towards him.

'Good morning, my love', she said in a still sleepy, bedroom voice that stirred Tom.

'Good morning.' Tom blew her a kiss.

'You woke me!'

'I didn't!' Tom protested. He had enjoyed watching her sleeping like an innocent, not making any sound, but savoring the view and permitting it to memory.

'I could feel your eyes on me, and that woke me!' There was no accusation, merely a simple statement.

Changing track, Tom inquired 'When did you leave? Last thing I remember, you were asleep in my arms...'

Theres sat up and tried her feet on the floor. It was cool against her bare soles, and she stood up with another luxurious, feline stretch. Tom remembered her purring the previous night. He was intent on making her purr again soon. Love for her and especially making love to her had become important and suddenly was uppermost in his mind.

'I woke up and there wasn't all that much space, so I decided to get into your bed. I thought we could both do with a good sleep.'

She lifted the curtains on his window, briefly disappearing from his view. The sun of an early summer morning set her skin aglow like pink marble. It lingered when she stepped back into his vision. 'You know, the train is not moving. We must be short of Paris, apparently they tell you before we get there, so you can be all dressed up when we pull into the station.' Tom did not care for her explanation. He wanted to see her naked, beautiful body near him, where he could touch and once more forget himself in her caresses and kisses.

She came strolling back closer to him, natural and confident in her nakedness. Theres seemed not at all self-conscious about her body, and he loved her for that, as much and maybe even more than for the way she made him feel. Every minute they spent together was like a breath of fresh, fragrant air on a warm summer evening, rejuvenating and blissful.

When she pulled the blanket off him, she saw his erection. Tom could not help but react to her presence in this way yet again. Thinking about the previous night had made him yearn for more of her. Theres smiled.

'Hello', she whispered, taking a hold of his erection and talking to it rather than to Tom. 'I remember you from last night. You have been doing well, my love, I enjoyed you!'

Tom touched the silken thigh closest to him and she did not move away. Wafts of pungent aroma engulfed him. He had not used preventives, and he had filled her time and again with his spawn. Since their encounter Theres had not showered and their combined juices had trickled down the inside of her legs all night long. He longed to kiss this flow of pleasure and happiness, but waited for her to move closer towards him.

Still holding on to his pride, Theres bent over and flicked her tongue over his precious and most sensitive part. Tom held his breath and closed his eyes. Her lips engulfed him as far down on his shaft as she could manage, forming a close grip. She pulled up and wetted the length of his shaft with her spittle. In response to Tom's moan of pleasure, she flicked her tongue once more over his perceptive glands before continuing to suck for just as long as it took Tom to recover his breath. His eyes were still shut when she moved and positioned her body over him. She straddled him and pushed his manhood to the gates of her heaven and bade him enter.

He entered and filled her. He was big enough to both stretch and satisfy her just by his presence. When she tilted her hips back and forth, she moved him inside herself just the tiniest of fractions, making the motion pleasurable and exquisite for both. This, she continued, rocking slowly and gently back and forth.

Her eyes sparkled in the light of the rising sun. It penetrated through a crack in the curtain, bathing the lovers in its glory and promise.

Theres leant forward and titillated Tom with dangling breasts too generous and bold to ignore. He willingly obliged and took hold of a joyful nipple with his teeth, carefully. She liked him to bite a little harder once the sexual tension built inside her. For just now, this was play, and he was gentle.

Theres tilted her hips once again, and pushed her moist pearl against his pubic bone. Her bare pussy was covered with the shortest of bristles, and he felt them caressing his mound coarsely. The sensation was erotic and exciting, and he hoped she would continue. Inside her he felt enclosed and constricted, the articulation of their bodies like another piston, another valve, in the engine of the Orient Express. He could stay like that forever.

He closed his eyes once more to savor the little pulses her presence startled all over him. His balls were once again filling with the excitement of an explosion not too far away, accumulating deep in his belly and ready to be released shortly, when suddenly, Theres stopped and sat up.

'We can't keep on doing this, you know!'

'Why? What is the matter?' Exasperation sounded in Tom's voice.

'We have plans, that is why!'

Theres jumped up and walked into the bathroom, where she turned on the shower. Tom could hear the water rushing and hitting the floor.

Through the sudden din, her voice called.

'I thought we could go for a walk. We have about six hours, and we can have breakfast somewhere near Montmartre, maybe overlooking the Seine. What do you think?'

'I think you should come right back here and finish what you started!'

'I will never finish with that, as you well know. Come on, get a move-on, there is a new day out there!'

She closed the door and Tom felt his erection collapse forlornly onto his belly. There was no stopping Theres and once she had an idea, she would see it through. But once again, he would go along with whatever her plans were, as so far, they had been extraordinary.

So was she, and even though he felt discontented about being so abruptly interrupted in his love making, he got up and went into his cabin.

Theres took her time to shower. When she was finished, the small bathroom was filled with steam and the fragrance of her shampoo and showergel. The smell of fresh citrus fruit hung in the air. Before returning to her cabin and drying off, she knocked on Tom's door to let him know that she was done and that it was his turn.

When Tom eventually showered and dressed, he returned to her room.

'You didn't say what was planned, so I just put on my every day gear. Want me to change?'

Theres was bending over her rucksack. She looked up at him. Her hair was still not dry and had curled into little ringlets that made him believe once again that she was an angel. He should not have worried about dressing up that morning: Theres was in cropped jeans and a purple top. Her feet were bare and she looked confused.

'I can't find the second shoe ... I know I packed it!'

Tom smiled.

'I am glad you are human, too. Are you sure it should be in there?'

'Of course', she snapped.

'There it is!'

Theres held out the opposite to a shoe that he had noticed on the floor. When she slipped them on, she was nearly as tall as him, so he looked again.

'Heels? I am surprised at you.'

'No heels, not really. I sure will not break an ankle in these, they are just heavy on the soles ... do you mind?'

Tom shook his head.

'No. You look wonderful to me, whatever you choose to wear. That color suits you. And I like your hair like that. You are beautiful!'

Theres smiled - her whole face radiated warmth and he could see the small, fine laughter lines around her green eyes. They flashed at him and he kissed her. In response, she wrapped her arms around his neck and nestled her face into his cheek.

'I love you, Tom. More than you ever will know. But now, it will soon be time to meet Paris and get some breakfast.'

For a moment, they rocked together from side to side, happy in the embrace and content with each other.

'What is going to happen with the luggage?' Tom suddenly inquired.

'What do you mean? What about the luggage?'

'If this is Paris, is this not our stop? You know, where we get off?'

Theres snapped her head back and laughed heartily. Stroking his face, she shook her head in disbelief before she explained:

'I didn't tell you, did I? WE are going to go ALL the WAY. This train is going to take us from Paris to Istanbul. We are staying another five days!'

Tom gasped. He had enjoyed the one night and now relished the idea that there would be five more. He kissed her again. Yet again, he was speechless. Theres explained:

'This, my wonderful, is a very special train, and not just because it is harboring you and me. They have only recently done the refurbishment, and this is the first trip where there is a first class compartment - ours, you know - with showers and single beds. And normally, it does not go all the way from London, this is unique, a one-off. And when we leave Paris, we go through Switzerland to Vienna, then on to Budapest, across Hungary into Rumania, through Transylvania, Bucharest and then onto Turkey. Like it?'

Tom nodded.

CHAPTER 5

Passengers had congregated in the various bars and dinner cars of the Orient Express when the train pulled into Paris. There was applause and a general good-natured and pleasant atmosphere. Some of the clientele said their good-byes as they only were booked on the first leg of the journey. Already, there were new faces waiting to board the train and share the luxury to Istanbul.

For a while, Tom and Theres looked on at the crowd outside. These people would be their new traveling companions, as they could not totally avoid mingling with the other passengers on the train. They watched and wondered which of these strangers they would meet on their way to the buffet car or restaurant, speak to and exchange pleasantries with. Theres and Tom waved at the men and women on the platform, but they were more excited about a few hours in Paris, the capitol of love, than anything else.

Theres hurriedly explained to one of the staff that they would spend a few hours in town, before returning around 3:30 for their afternoon teas. She pulled Tom outside as soon as the doors were opened. Making their way through the general hustle of the station, they could not avoid a woman hurrying towards them, all colorful, flowing caftans and clicking heels. A porter tried bravely to keep up with her, but struggled along under a heavy load. In the small coming-together, Theres' purse fell to the floor and the woman huffed at her impatiently.

'I am in a rush, I have a train to catch', was all she said. She spoke with an American accent, and Tom frowned. There was no apology, and under normal circumstances, Theres would have objected and complained, but she was too happy and Tom was with her. Tom bent to pick up her small bag. Theres stood and followed the woman with her eyes. Then she shook her head in disbelief at the rudeness she had encountered, but banished any further thoughts about the incident from her mind. Today, she was in Paris and with Tom, and that meant so much more to her.

They made their way to a taxi stand, where Theres began a discussion with a driver in what seemed to Tom to be fluent French. When they slid into the back seat, he whispered

'I didn't know you spoke the language?'

Theres shrugged.

'Enough to order a taxi driver to take us where we can have breakfast, and where we can see the Seine at the same time. Didn't I promise you that?'

The trip lasted only a few minutes, but Tom did not have eyes for the scenery outside. He held Theres' hand firmly in his own and marveled at the feelings she evoked deep within him. He had lied to his family to spend this time with this fascinating young woman, and he knew he should have regrets, but there were none. On the contrary, he realized that if he had told her that he could not come along, he would have regretted that decision for the rest of his life. This was where he needed to be, with Theres, his Theres. He never wanted to be without this woman again. Tears shot into his eyes, and he quickly tried to pull himself together. But she had seen, and it was her hand that wiped the tears away.

'It will be alright', she whispered when she kissed the hand that was holding hers.

Breakfast in the small, predominantly French café had been excellent. Fresh croissants, and coffee from large, generous mugs, steaming and almost too hot to drink. They had chatted, about inconsequential matters, and they had laughed together. Gone were the dark clouds from earlier, and both enjoyed the repartee and closeness.

Later, they walked hand in hand along the Seine, mingling with the other lovers. Ever so often, one would point at a nice building, or a cute dog, or a tourist boat on the river. At other times, they would stop and kiss. The air smelled of summer heat and the sun warmed their faces. They were happy and relaxed.

'O look, street artists!'

Theres pulled him across the street. They had reached the artist's quarter where the painters were sketching the scenery or passers-by. One young man stood up when Theres and Tom approached. He urged her to sit for him, and Theres shot a quick glance at Tom.

'Please, go ahead. I would like a picture of you.'

Tom pushed her onto the chair the man had proffered, and then he watched as a few hurried strokes of paint on the paper started to bring Theres' face to life. How he desired for the artist to capture her beauty for him! Theres had taken her glasses off and smiled at the young man, opening her lips just enough to flash her perfect set of teeth.

'I will be just over there', Tom suddenly said and disappeared before Theres could protest for him to wait for her.

A few minutes went by and Tom was back by her side. He held a small parcel.

'Just a small water color of the river', he explained. He looked pleased.

The picture of Theres succeeded as he had hoped. She paid the asking price in French francs and Tom gave him a ten-dollar bill. Theres wanted to object, but he shook her off.

'No, no, the man has done well. He has created a beautiful painting of a beautiful woman, and I want to honor that.'

At three o'clock, Theres hailed a taxi and they returned to the train station. The Orient Express sat on a special platform, people around it, and waiting for leaving time to come, to proceed at a slow pace south and east toward Istanbul.

They boarded in silence. After refreshing briefly in their cabins, they went to the buffet car for afternoon tea.

At four o'clock exactly, there was a commotion outside. A young woman was walking along the train and calling out for someone. Heads turned. Theres leant towards the window to see what evolved. Tom focused his eyes on his teacup.

'What is going on?' he asked.

'There is some woman outside, seems she is looking for someone.'

When the woman came closer, Theres suddenly heard her own name called – 'Madame Theres from Aberdeen'. There could be no misunderstanding, the woman's accent was clear enough. Theres flushed when she looked at Tom. His eyes beamed at her, and suddenly it dawned on her that he had something to do with the woman calling her name.

'What have you been up to? Tom?'

He shook his head.

'Go and see, my love, go on...'

Theres got up. Other passengers around them followed her with their eyes. She felt slightly embarrassed. Pink cheeks suited her. Tom put down his napkin and was a step behind her when she reached the door to the platform. Theres waved at the woman. The woman quickly made her way towards her.

'Madame Theres from Aberdeen?' she inquired.

'Yes, that is me.'

The woman carried a heavy basket. She bent to lift out a bouquet of two dozen red and pink roses, wrapped in cellophane, and with a card stuck out at the top. This, the woman now held out for Theres.

'I don't ... understand ...' Theres muttered.

Tom thanked the young woman, paid her a tip and grabbed hold of Theres' arm.

She looked at him, still speechless.

'Tom', was all she could muster.

'I love you. No more primroses between us from now on, I want there to be nothing but roses. Roses of love. Roses for my angel.'

Theres threw her free arm around him, pressing the roses between their bodies, holding on tight. People started to applaud. There were cheers. Neither of them cared.

'I love you, Thomas, I love you. Nobody has ever done anything like this for me, ever. I love you so much.'

When she let go of him, Tom guided her back onto the train. A waiter stood by with a large vase to take the bouquet from her hands and to arrange the flowers for her in her cabin. When they came into Theres' room, the fragrance was so sensuous that they stood, holding on to each other, gaining strength from only each other's presence.

CHAPTER 6

The train had pulled out of Paris Gare de l'Est a few minutes late, but then deliberately and purposefully shuckled its way through the suburbs. Bye and bye, the sounds of afternoon tea being served in the cabins died down; the train settled into the wait for dinner. Muffled voices from the other passengers made their way into their cabin. These sounds were comforting and peaceful.

Theres and Tom had decided to rest a little and when she returned from a short nap in her room, she found him sitting at the small table, an empty cup in front of him. His brow was furrowed and he focused on the far distance. The sun had almost settled on the horizon, and the room was drenched in the last rays. He was unaware of her presence, and she remained to watch him for the length of a breath or two. The warm feeling that always surrounded her and crept up inside her whenever she was near him, took hold once more. She knew she was deeply in love with Tom, despite the circumstances. He had grown to be a most important part of her life within an extraordinary short span of time, and she was glad they were together.

'Tom?'

He looked up. A smile flickered over his face, but he avoided looking into her eyes. He turned back to the window and his observation of the country limbering by in the early evening sun.

'Come and join me', he offered.

Theres took the chair opposite him. His hands came to meet her, but she refused the touch. Instead, she searched his face, but did not find any easy answers.

'Tom?'

'Yes, dear?'

'Tom, what did you tell your wife about where you are?'

Tom took a deep breath and faced her.

'Am I this transparent to you?'

'I love you, and your thoughts may not be too distant from mine. You were lost in thought, and it did not seem to be a happy one, so I wondered...' the end of her sentence hung in the air like particles of dust. Tom did not need to hear her finish to know what she was thinking. Their few days together had been magic. They had been happy, but it was a stolen happiness, one that could not last much past their holiday together. It would always be this way, unless...

'I told Lillian that I was traveling. Alone. And that it might be difficult to find the time to phone her. She has no idea, at least I think she hasn't, about me being with someone else, another woman.'

'You know, people will find our relationship sordid and dirty.'

'I love you.'

'And I love you, but still, we both have others in our lives. And that, eventually, will cause problems. And hurt to either us or them.'

Tom took hold of her hands and held them tightly within his. He could not look at her, and the thoughts topmost in his mind were painful. He knew she was right.

'I know what it must look like for other people. Sordid - well ... dirty - I am a married man, more than twenty years your senior. You are a beautiful woman with a career and an absentee husband. I am retired, you have a life to live. I love you and I know that since I first came across you. I have been wondering where this would end, could end. I don't want it to end. I want to love you till I die, and then some!'

His voice had grown in vehemence. It was obvious to her that he meant every word. Theres felt torn, torn between running into his arms to forget about this exchange and dragging it all in the open. Openness won.

'I told Ben that I am visiting with some girlfriends before I am off to the States. And that I was moving around too much for him to phone from the ship. He doesn't suspect either.'

Silence descended. Outside, a happy shiny sun went to bed, bathing the countryside in layers of red and orange. The cabin fell into late-evening dimness, but neither of them stirred to turn on the light. They hardly breathed. It was Tom who broke the silence.

He stood up and from his jacket on a hook behind the door, he extracted his wallet. When he returned to the table and Theres, he proffered her two photographs.

'My daughter, Jenny, and my granddaughter, Megan. These past few years, I have lived for them. I love them deeply and I could not bear to hurt them.'

Theres looked at two smiling, beautiful faces that stared up at her from the photographs. She had known about them, known that Tom had a house full of women at home whom he doted upon and who ruled his life. Whenever he spoke of his daily affairs, it was these two he talked of. She hardly knew anything about Lillian.

'I don't know whether I ever could leave them.'

'Is that what you were thinking about when I came in?'

'Yes, it was. Before I came to meet you, I wasn't sure. All I wanted was a little time with you and to see how we would get on once we met in the flesh, so to speak. That no longer will be enough.'

There were tears in his eyes.

'Theres, I am torn. I love my girls. And I love you.'

When he eventually turned to look at her once more, she could see the plea for help in his eyes. But there was nothing she could do to give him comfort.

'I never thought that leaving your family was part of the deal. I just wanted to be with you, and I thought that was what you wanted. A dalliance. The primrose path of Hamlet and Ophelia. When I am in Detroit, things will be easier for us, you can jump in the car and come and visit me whenever possible. I never thought you were contemplating ... more.'

'If I wanted more, if I was to leave, would you have me? Would you leave Ben and live with me?'

'You know Ben and I are having difficulties. But I love him. Maybe in a way different from the way I love you, but he needs me. And when it comes to it, he is not bad as husbands go. I honestly don't know.'

Silence descended once again. It was laden with deep thoughts, thoughts that were almost physical and hung dark and weighty over them for a while.

'I love you, Tom. Every day I wake up and there is you. Every day, when I go to work, I think of you and I smile to myself. My day has purpose. Time drags till I can go home, and the first thing I usually do is to check for emails from you. Then I log onto the chatroom and wait for you. The time we spend is the most precious time to me, any day without you is wasted. You give me motivation, it is the thought of you that powers me on. You are my purpose. Maybe I will leave Ben, but that will not depend on what you decide. Maybe I leave Ben because he does not touch me like you do. Ben is physical, not deep down like you. I can't describe this feeling you give me, but I feel whole with you. And now, that we are on this journey together, all my dreams of you are coming true. I love you, Tom, no matter what you decide or the future will bring.'

Tom smiled quietly and squeezed her hands once more.

'You don't know what it does to me when you say this. I feel so ... honored that I am the one that makes you feel this happy. It also makes me feel so humble that you should trust in me this much. I love you, and I never want to stop saying it.'

He took a deep and labored breath before he continued.

'Our outside life is part of us, and I believe neither of us can hide from that. Let us concentrate on each other while we have the chance. Theres, all my life, I have wanted someone to touch me like you do - touch me spiritually, intellectually, not only physically. You are an inspiration, you are full of magic, and whenever I think I know all about you and how you would react to something I do or say, you surprise me and I see you in light ever-changing. Each time you become more perfect, more beautiful. I love you. I love you. I love you.'

'And at the same time, you are wondering what Lillian is doing right now.'

'That is not fair!' Tom tugged at her hands. His face mirrored the hurt her simple statement had caused.

'Sorry. I am so happy to have you here, to spend this time together, and at the same time, I am already sad to know it will end soon.'

'Don't be. Let us make a pact, right now. Let us promise to enjoy the time we have. Let us learn to concentrate on nothing but each other. Yes, there will be times when I think about Lillian and my daughter and granddaughter, but this time now belongs to you!'

'Tom?'

'Yes, dear?'

'I love you.'

He stood up and pulled her close, to enshrine her in his arms, holding her as close as possible. Their heartbeats joined and pulsated together with new strength, making their love tactual. The scent of the roses spilled into their minds and hearts, and they greedily drank in the heady aroma.

The spell of the moment was broken when a knock from the corridor made them jolt apart. The waiter brought their dinner and they ate in near silence, each hanging after his own thoughts.

CHAPTER 7

They were drinking coffee, when Tom suddenly began to swallow with effort.

'Are you alright?' Theres watched him with concern.

'My throat is sore. It hurts when I swallow.'

'Just now?'

'Well, now that you are asking, it was a bit sore when we came back to the train in Paris. You don't think I have caught a throat infection or something?'

Theres shrugged. 'Could be. Do you get sore throats easily?'

Tom nodded. 'I think I better have an early night tonight and wrap up well. Do you mind?'

Disappointment was written on her face, and it nearly broke his heart. The earlier talk still overlaid their thoughts and he didn't want her to think that his feelings for her had changed in any way.

'No, that is fine. You make sure you are better soon, that is more important.'

She was about to leave his cabin, when she turned around and looked at him. She still looked worried.

'Do you want to go back home early?'

'Theres - NO!' in disbelief, he looked at her. With only two steps, he was with her, embracing her and pressing her face against his shoulder. 'No, my love, no, no', he whispered, comforting her like a child.

Theres stood up straight, looked into his eyes, kissed him goodnight and smiled shyly.

'I love you.'

CHAPTER 8

Tom could hear her rummage around her cabin - thankfully she had closed both the doors. Eventually, there was silence and he hoped she would be asleep. From the near-by bar car, he could faintly make out the sound of the piano. They had debated about joining the other passengers, but had decided that they wanted to be by themselves.

Quietly, trying not to make any sound, he heaved her suitcase into his cabin and closed the door - better to keep two closed doors between them, just to make sure.

He lay her case flat onto his upturned bed and opened it. There were clothes he had not seen her wear before; the one that he liked most was a white dress that he took out to examine in detail.

She must only recently have bought this frock, as there still was a tag in the seam. It smelled of her already, maybe because it had been confined with her other clothes. He shook the dress to its full extent and held it against his bulk. It was near to floor-length. The top was crocheted and would fit tightly around her full round breasts. The skirt was wide and flouncy. It would make her look even more like an angel. His angel, no matter what doubts he might have about their future together.

Tom turned and caught his reflection in the mirror. 'You old fool', he said to himself. 'Make sure that you look after her. She is worth a hundred of you, and never you forget that!'

He breathed in deeply, drinking in the essence of Theres, given to him by her clothes. He hugged the soft material closer, imagining that she was already wearing it. His skin prickled and he desired her.

He closed his eyes and could see her wearing that dress, in his arms, and he could imagine the smell of her hair and the freshness of her skin against his chest when she nestled there, holding on to him like the child he yearned to protect. Theres, his Theres. Lillian or no, Theres he would never leave, she would always be in his heart and every waking moment would be filled with memories of her.

Tom returned from his reveries when the train halted. He quickly changed into his slacks, closed Theres' suitcase before returning it to its rest, and then knocked at her door. He entered almost at the same moment and threw the white dress at her.

'Put that on and come to my cabin. Hurry!' He barked at her. Then he withdrew.

A minute later, Theres stood in his cabin, her feet bare and her hair tousled. But she wore the white dress. Angel. She was confused and he signaled her to remain quiet. Then, he led her out into the corridor. Nobody else seemed around. A silent valet nodded at them when they slid past him. The doors to the outside were open. Cool night air greeted them and Tom put his arm around Theres to shelter her from the breeze. He shunted her out and she could feel moist blades of grass under her feet. Tom maneuvered her around a small gate and along a hedge. When they turned again, she could make out faint lights. Lanterns had been placed along their path. A soft, light-colored blanket had been spread for them, a cooler held a bottle of dark green glass, two tall glass flutes rested against a small basket holding fresh fruit, and cushions were scattered around.

Theres was stunned. She had worried about the nocturnal activities, wondered what was going on, but she trusted Tom and knew that he would not let her come to harm. Tom felt the pride of a young man, impressing his first love with his ingenuity. He physically felt his happiness.

'You said it was a special train, didn't you?'

'Tom, what have you done? This is ... wonderful!'

'Well, my angel, you are not the only one who can organize things. Now sit down. The train is only stopping for forty minutes, and before long, you will feel the cold.'

Theres lowered herself onto the cushions and took the flutes. They were heavier than she had expected, and when she realized that they were of fine crystal, she was astounded. This was pure, unadulterated luxury and she began to enjoy the moment, despite the cold seeping through the night and making her skin tingle. Tom uncorked the Champagne.

'Here is to our love - and to eternity.'

'Here is to the moon and stars.'

'Here is to love.'

'Here is to you and me!'

The cork flew into the night. Flutes filled, they clinked the crystal and created a sound that rang like music in the air. Theres remembered that some famous prima donna could shatter crystal with the pitch of her voice, and she giggled. She wished she could sing, but she just smiled and moved closer towards Tom. Before they drank, their lips met joyfully. Forgotten were the darker thoughts from earlier. Their love would surmount any hurdles and objections, as long as they could steal these moments.

'I didn't have a sore throat at all, I needed to make sure you would be asleep by yourself. I wanted to surprise you. Have I done well?'

Theres giggled. The Champagne had bubbled into her nose and the cool liquid tickled her throat.

'You are wonderful, my love. And yes, you have done well. I am impressed. But how did you know about this stop? How did you manage to organize this ... picnic?'

She looked around, marveling at the scrumptiousness of the simple setting.

'I spoke to the valet earlier on, he happened to mention a stop of an hour or so. They have to wait for a train from the other direction, as from here there is only a single line for a while. I asked him whether we could arrange a midnight picnic, and he had no problems with that. We are the only first class passengers, so they were keen to oblige. And who knows, maybe in future, they will take this into their program. But for now, my love, there is just you and me and a train full of nosy waiters looking on. Come here, kiss me.'

He pulled her close, spilling some of the sparkling wine. They kissed and snuggled up to each other. Theres' dress did not hold out the cold, and he rubbed her bare arms to keep them warm. For a while, they lay next to each other, looking up at the stars and relishing their togetherness. He would never forget the way she looked that night, and the way she made him feel.

The same silent valet from earlier came to tell them that they would have to leave soon. Tom stood up first, and pulled Theres to her feet. Then, flutes in their hands, they returned to the train and their cabin. Somebody would tidy up after them; they were only concerned with themselves.

'I am cold', Theres whispered when they were alone in her compartment. 'Just hold me a little.' She pressed herself into his arms, and Tom happily obliged. He had lost all sense of time, and he wanted to remain there with her as long as possible.

'Sit down, my love, I'll get a hot towel and rub your feet.'

While he went to the bathroom, Theres turned on some quiet music. Her mp3 player still operated after she changed out the batteries, and classical music soothed and suited the atmosphere of this night. The cabin filled with the sound of strings flooding and ebbing like waves on a seashore.

When Tom reentered the room, Theres had made herself comfortable on the bed, propping her back against some cushions. Her feet dangled, waiting for his caresses.

Tom stooped and bent down on his knees. Gently, he took first one foot and then the other and rubbed them into the hot and moist towel he had brought from the bathroom. He folded up her dress to her knees and gently massaged her ankles and calves with the towel. Theres sighed and closed her eyes.

'Mhm, I like that', she whispered.

'Want me to continue?' he asked, matching her whisper. His ministrations aroused him, and he knew where he wanted them to lead.

'As long as you like', Theres spoke softly. She, too, was aware of the erotic nature of his touch. Memories of the previous night and morning came rushing back. His touch had been gentle, at the same time demanding and giving. Their love-making had been special and there was more to come.

Tom stroked farther up her legs. The towel was still warm and just a little rough against her thighs. When he lifted her dress a little more, he gasped.

'No wonder you are cold! Where are your panties?'

Theres giggled. 'You only told me to put the dress on. Couldn't find panties in a hurry, so ...'

Tom leant into her and buried his face between her legs. He so longed to kiss her, gently and passionately, but the aroma overwhelmed him. It was the aroma of the sea, of fresh oysters, a heady mix, the essence of him interspersed with that of her. He lapped at her thighs, and then kissed her pleasure pearl gently.

'Does it taste nice down there?' she asked and he grunted. He had not wanted to do this, but now that he sat before her, his eyes feasting on the views she offered, he could not help himself. Her bared lips hid the dark secret of her sex, but the little shiny pearl stuck out, asking him to take care of it lovingly.

His tongue flicked over her preciousness and she moaned. He heard her whispers - whispers that drove him to explore. He caressed her thighs, and then slipped one finger into the dark tunnel, like a miniature Orient Express, luxurious but focused. He revolved his finger and felt her hips moving in response. This turned her on as much as it pleasured him, and he continued.

He sucked her clit and she urged him to continue. 'Keep going, keep going'. He needed no more encouragement.

Her pearl was big and shiny, and he sucked at it gently at first, then with more intensity as he sensed her body tightening. Against all hope, he wished he could make her cum like this. He probed her inner vagina, increasing the friction of his fingers in those accordion pleats of wet velvet.

'Don't stop, please don't stop', she suddenly whimpered. He wanted to be inside her, to spawn more salmon in the upper tributaries, but he knew she would not forgive him if he stopped now. 'Please' she whimpered again, panting and throwing her head around. Suddenly, with brutal force, her whole body contracted. His face was crushed between her thighs, her mound pressed against his face. She groaned and shrieked, and felt the surging pulse as she contracted powerfully around his fingers. Her hands pulled him towards her, pulling and tugging at his hair. Her climax lasted for seconds and afterwards, she laughed hysterically.

'Come here, you, and make love to me ... again....' She pulled his head towards her face, smelling her own sanctum, and then tasted his lips with hers. Tom's erection was harder than ever before and found its way into Theres. They fell back onto the bed, lips and bodies entwined and made love, again.

CHAPTER 9

'Do you know this area?'

The train wound its way slowly through valleys surrounded by mountaintops. Over night, the scenery had changed and they had traveled from France with ripe fields of wheat into Switzerland with its cool forests and mountains, and now were on their way into Austria. At least, Theres thought they were.

'Not really', she threw in. 'I grew up north of here, and spent my teenage years on the northern side of Lake Constance. The German side. I traveled in Switzerland and Austria just a little bit, and mainly when we had foreign visitors – you know, living in a famous tourist area and showing off at how nice and neat it all is. I never was into skiing, so there wasn't all that much of a need to go into the mountains.'

The views outside their windows were magnificent. On top of the mountains, there still was snow. It reflected brilliantly the beams of yet another full and warming summer sun. Their train ran through picture-postcard-perfect villages. But their train didn't stop, so they could not indulge their romantic nature and go for a walk, hand in hand along the clean ridges. Theres opened the compartment window slightly and cool, fresh air spilled in. They had breakfasted in the dining car, but there had been too many others to sit and talk; and as they intended to make the most of their time together, they had gone back to their own suite of cabins. There they sat at the window, looking out.

'Is the German side different from this? I have never been there, so I am interested. And the fact that you know first hand … I am just curious and want to know all you can tell me.'

Theres had to smile. Tom had been an interesting travel companion so far, but she gave him the most pleasure when she shared her knowledge. Of course, they shared other pleasures, just as important, but far more private than her experience of travelling Europe.

'I used to travel into Austria, just over the border and maybe five minutes down the road to the next town. Bregenz, that is. You might have heard of this place, as every summer, they have these concerts on the Lake, with the stage sitting out on the water and people looking on from the shore. Anyway, what I wanted to tell you is this: all that separates the two countries is an arbitrary line which defined that one side of it is Austrian, and the other is German. But as soon as you crossed the line, things were different, and noticeably so. Even people looked different, and they certainly spoke different. Probably still do!'

Theres took a breath and looked out for a moment before returning to her discourse.

'I think that deep down, Germans have a problem with both the Swiss and especially the Austrians. I remember growing up, knowing that the Swiss were the Scots of Continental Europe, a bit uppity and proud of their money-business, and the Austrians were smarmy and you couldn't trust them, ever. I often wondered whether the Germans still blamed the Austrians for Hitler, but then I am not sure. You see, I only ever traveled across the border when we had visitors that wanted showing around. Have you heard of the Rhine Falls?'

Tom's thoughts were still trying to interpret Theres' view on European politics. Her mind skipped from topic to topic, and he was glad that they were back on travel and tourism. Discussing politics with Theres meant that he listened and she talked; he knew that he could not hold his own with her strong opinions. He would not want it any other way and relished these exchanges.

'The Rhine Falls?'

'Yes. They are in Switzerland. You asked me about rivers, a long time ago. I can't quite see your fascination with rivers, I am much more a sea-type of person, but then, the Rhine I think is quite important to me. I was born further north, not far from the Rhine Valley where they have all that gorgeous German wine, and later, I lived near the Lake Constance, which is fed by the Rhine. In Switzerland, there is like a mini Niagara, not quite as splendid, but nevertheless. There are a few nice niches around there, and maybe one day, we can go and I show you. That can't be far from where the train passes. I wish I had a map!'

The chair rattled against the window frame when Theres stood up with force. She was restless, as so often, when her mind flitted from one idea to the next. He had noticed this energy before; she was unstoppable when she had something on her mind. She was like a train, running along on a track leading to whatever it was she focused on that instant. Right now, it was a map.

'Back in a mo', was the last thing he heard when she left the room in search for a waiter or valet - and a map.

Outside, the scenery had changed yet again. The train pushed its way through a forest. Even through the din of the engine, Tom believed he could hear the birds sing brightly. Theres was gone but a minute, and yet he yearned for her to come back. He felt silly, but at the same time, he knew he was in love. In love like a teenager. He needed her by his side, as that was where she belonged. Theres did not need him, he had realized that a long time ago, before he ever had come to meet her in Scotland, all that time ago - four days? Five already? Time had blurred. There was just Theres. And maybe it wasn't the birds that were singing, maybe it was his own heart. He didn't care. The sun shone, and it would shine inside of him, even in the greatest downpour outside, in the most terrible hurricane, all because of her!

She returned, unfolding a map of middle Europe, covering Switzerland, Austria and parts of Hungary. She smoothed the paper onto the little table, and carefully pointed to a corner on the south-westerly side of Lake Constance.

'Rhine Falls.'

She stood next to Tom, and her closeness took his breath away. She smelled clean and fresh, and exactly like a woman should. With his arm around her waist, he pulled her onto his knees.

'Come and sit with me and show me where you went to school.'

'For a while, I went to school in a town on the German side of the lake. That was nice - at least most of the time. The school wasn't too hot, and I didn't make an effort. There were nearly forty kids in my class, and it was easy to fall by the wayside. I remember that for a whole term I never turned up for sports, and only once or twice for physics. Don't look at me like that! I admit it, I was a truant and absconder!'

Tom had not looked at her directly, but her mocking tone made him concentrate on the map just a little more. A smile ran across his face and he hugged her close in response.

'Town was exciting. I had to travel by bus, as we lived a few miles outside town, and the bus park was right at the lake. In summer, there were hordes of tourists, and it was always busy. It also would get extremely hot and that I didn't like. But it was fun. And we would go to bathe in the lake, I loved that. Not quite like an ocean, but cool and fresh. One year, there were loads of dead fish. You see, every four or five years, they would all just die, I don't know why. That was disgusting. One of my pals stood on one and it was all squishy and stank. I don't have to tell you that I didn't go swimming much that year, do I?'

The train had changed direction and mid-morning sunshine gleamed through the window. Theres squinted. She had not been wearing her glasses that morning, and the bright light hurt her eyes. She shifted on Tom's knees and embraced his head. She pulled him close and gently kissed him.

'Tell me more', Tom pleaded.

Theres looked at him and he could see the green flecks in her eyes that brought her face so alive. She smiled that smile that he was sure men could die for ... he was sure he would be willing to die for ... and a rush of warmth and excitement came over him. He pulled her lips onto his and gently forced his tongue into the cavity of her mouth. For a moment, they sat like that, before she pulled free.

'What would you like to know?'

'Anything you are willing to tell me!'

'And if I tell you that I love you?'

'That is one of the things I want to hear forever! But tell me more, please!'

'Shall I tell you that I think you are wonderful?'

'Tell me that if you like, but I was hoping for a little more about our journey.'

'Would you like me to tell you where we are going next? And where we are going to spend tonight?'

'Would you tell me that?'

'No. It is going to be a surprise. But I am sure that if you wanted to find out, you could have looked at the itinerary that is hanging up there.' Theres pointed to the folder Tom had found the previous night, which held all the information about their journey. The temptation had been too much, and he had had to have a peek. He knew that they were going past Vienna and would spend the night in Budapest.

'Tell me about Vienna then.'

'You cheat - you DID peek!' Theres kissed him again. Then she resumed her former position on his knees and continued with her views of her world.

'There is not much I can tell you about Vienna. I have never been there. Once, I knew someone who came from there. He taught at summer school and he was real proud of the place. One of the other women that attended, a German woman, had been to see some opera performed there, and she had spent a few days in the place, and she told him how dirty and disgusting and run-down she had found it. I think he realized that this was the picture a lot of people had, but he loved Vienna and he loved being there. He just crumpled under her criticism. I felt so sorry for him!'

'Did you love that man?'

'O no, what an absurd idea! He was a lecturer, and he was quite young. You know I prefer slightly older men. And men that are not Austrian - I told you, I grew up with an unhealthy distrust of all things Austrian!' Theres chuckled. Tom's question had been absurd, she had no feelings for the lecturer. In her mind, though, she still could see that young man and his anguish at the way the woman had bad-mouthed his beloved city.

'I always wanted to see the white horses. But I never went, I don't think we could have afforded it.'

'You told me before that money had been tight when you grew up. But your parents had good jobs, didn't they?'

'Mum had - but for most of what I can remember, her choice of partner had not always been ... successful. And she never was any good with money herself. She never managed to save anything, so she forever chased her debts. So, there was no money ever for holidays. I was in my twenties before I ever went and spent a night in a hotel!'

For a while, they sat silent. Silence between them was never uncomfortable. Silence meant that they took breath for the next, new topic of their conversation. Silence was the time for a kiss or an embrace. Silence was when they watched together, experiencing the same sensations, breathing the same air and smelling the same scent.

'I don't like these mountains much, so I never wanted to travel and explore them. Has to do with my migraines.'

'Hmm - I didn't catch that. How did we get from the mountains to your migraines?'

'That goes back to when I was a teenager and went to school north of here. You see, there is this weather phenomenon called 'Foen'. Same word as the German for 'hairdrier'. You get that when there is a warm wind from the south, if I remember correctly. During foen, you always could see the Swiss mountains very clearly. It was as though they were right close, as if you could just stretch out your hand and touch them. You could see the snow on the mountain tops, really picturesque. It meant that I didn't even need to get up - I was sick with yet another migraine. Sometimes, I wouldn't be able to get up for days.'

'How are you now?' Concern swung in his voice. She had told him about her migraines, and he was not sure what to do should she fall ill.

'I am fine. I haven't had an attack for over a year now, and I have some special medicine, so don't worry. And I hope there won't be any foen for the next few days!'

She kissed him once more before she stood up.

'Fancy dressing for lunch? I have seen the menu, it is absolutely delicious. So far, they have surpassed all my expectations, these chefs are masterly. Shall we honor them with suit and posh frock?' She smiled. Theres was right, so far, the food had been extremely scrumptious and Tom was once again happy to oblige.

'Suit and frock it is then.'

'Give me ten minutes and I get changed.'

When she reached the cabin door, he called her name and she turned around.

'I love you, Theres.' She smiled again when she left for her own compartment.

CHAPTER 10

Lunch was a superb affair, yet again. They feasted on salmon and delicate spring vegetables, washed down with a fruity Riesling from the Rhine Valley that Theres had chosen and which accompanied the tender and succulent fish superbly. Tom had learned to trust her sense for perfection, and this meal was no exception. His Theres had class, and it showed.

Vienna came and passed while they were having coffee. The train did not stop and they did not feel as though they were missing out. Maybe on another occasion, they could come back. Theres suggested they could hire one of those traditional horse-drawn carriages they offered and be shown the sights. That would have been very romantic and entirely appropriate. Tom would not have minded, it would have gone along with his romantic notions of their love.

Within a short while, Budapest loomed. Here, they were to stop overnight. Theres had mentioned that she had planned some kind of surprise for him, apart from other arranged activities. Tom did not mind, he looked forward to whatever she had thought out. As with the food and wine, he now knew he could trust her and her sense for the theatrical complemented his to perfection. That was it - maybe she had organized a visit to the opera or a concert. Whatever, he was bound to be delighted.

Once the train stopped, a porter collected their overnight baggage. They had been assured that there was no need to take all their cases with them. Valuables were locked away into the train's safe; all cabins were secured and several of the staff remained on-board to guarantee safety.

A taxi took Tom and Theres to a hotel south of the castle and close to the Danube, where first class accommodation awaited them.

Their room was de luxe. Thick carpets underfoot made up the first impression when they were led in to their suite. The room was in darkness, and when the light was turned on, they found themselves in a lounge decorated in an old-fashioned style, with heavy floral wallpaper above dark wooden wainscoting. A crystal chandelier focused the guests' eyes to the ceiling and detailed stucco. A basket full of fresh fruit and chocolates stood on a small mahogany table next to a door which led to their bedroom - a room mastered by a bed as large as neither of them had ever seen before. As soon as the bellboy had left them, Theres swung herself onto this bed. She bounced lasciviously.

'O, this is fantastic', she exclaimed. 'I have never been in a place like this! Tom, tell me, is this heaven?'

Tom joined her on the bed and leant over her to kiss her. 'I sure hope so', he whispered breathlessly.

Theres rolled away from him.

'There must be a bathroom as well', she called out as she walked through another door. 'Yep, here it is! Come and see this!'

Tom followed. Together, they stood in a wonderfully shiny, modern bathroom. Sink, stacks of towels, a bath, and a separate small compartment with the toilet and a bidet; the white fittings were offset by a dark marble floor and it smelled clean and fresh. But the most amazing thing in this bathroom was the shower cubicle. Whoever had designed this must have known that showers in luxurious hotel rooms would be used by more than one person at a time. It sat in a corner, and two of its sides were marble tiles. The other two were frosted glass panels and one of them opened outwards to allow entry. This access now stood open and they could see nozzles not only from one direction at the top, but also from two jets on either wall. Theres smiled happily.

'Don't you feel dirty and sweaty after all this travel? Don't you think a hot shower would be just the thing?'

She had already started to take her clothes off, and Tom followed keenly. Her exuberance and excitement infected him, and he needed to be close to her. As close as a hot shower and scented bath oils would allow.

The water was hot and they stood in the all-around jets. Water splashed at them from all angles. Steam and spray enveloped them. Theres slung her arms around Tom, kissing him. She stood so close that there was no room for any water to get in between them. Their lips pressed as their bodies intertwined and became one. Through the heat, Tom felt his body shiver. His physical need for her was obvious and Theres spread her thighs slightly to accommodate his erection against her mound. She tilted her head against his chin, and they stood, water and steam pouring over them; drinking in their physicality and proximity, at the same time yearning for more and not wanting to break the spell. Tom gave in first.

'Let's get out of here', he growled.

Theres turned the water off and opened the door. Cold from the bathroom hit them and both began to shiver. Theres grabbed the two largest bathsheets, took Tom by the hand, and led him into the bedroom. She spread the towels on the bed, and pointed for Tom to lie on one of them. But he moved in behind her, and turned her to face him.

He cupped her face in his hands and kissed her gently, before slowly going down on his knees, letting his lips stroke her skin as he did so. His hands pulled her close into him, so that his face rested against her pubic bone. He breathed in deeply. Fresh from the shower, her sex was moist from fluids other than water. She yearned for him as much as he did for her. Gently, he grasped the backs of her legs and drew them apart as she stood there. His tongue flickered gently over her shiny pearl before exploring deeper and finding the edge of the tunnel. Theres moaned. She wanted him there, ministering to her needs, and yet she also wanted his body on top of her, pinning her down under his weight and making love to her.

He caressed her silently. There were still trickles of moisture, little drops of water lazily congregated and formed larger drops to eventually fall onto the carpet. When his hands discovered the scrumptious roundness of her rear, he pulled her even closer and she nearly stumbled. She clung to his head and grabbed a fistful of hair. Her pulling excited him. With his face still hiding in her treasure trove, his hands once again journeyed north to cup her full breasts. Her nipples were erect, the aureola around them swollen and harshly rippled. His fingers tweaked and fumbled, and Theres squealed. The sensation of her flesh against his fingers was divine. She reacted the way he expected her to, and the fragrance emanating from her sex became more pungent and took hold of his senses.

He lifted himself up and grabbed her below her shoulder blades. Then he bent her slightly backwards and she sank onto his thighs. Their mouths met and their tongues instantly entwined the way he had come to cherish so.

The room was silent. Only the lapping of tongues and gentle cries of pleasure and sexual excitement affirmed the beauty and intensity of life. Theres lifted herself up to allow Tom to slide into her. They rocked back and forth, his legs supporting her, and her legs embracing him in a tight embrace.

The air in the room was still and gently warm, and shiny little beads of sweat glistened on their bodies. When Theres became aware of the salty moisture on his forehead, she carefully collected all the little droplets with her tongue.

'I love you', he whispered. 'I want to die in your arms tonight.'

'Shh', was all she replied. She kissed him once more, gently this time, before she leaned back and bared her breasts to him. Tom buried his face in the ampleness of her cleavage, before sucking first one, then the other, of her loud and sensuous nipples. They played, rocking gently back and forth in the ever-deepening rhythm of their passion as the Orient Express continued its passage ever further eastward.

'I have never yet felt you come with my prick inside you', Tom eventually whispered. 'What do I have to do to get you there?'

Theres hugged him close.

'Do you mind if I touch myself and you just make sure you stay inside?'

Tom had been aware, even though their lovemaking had been wonderfully gentle and of an unbelievable purity, that Theres had always seemed to hold back. He knew that she could be extremely violent and vocal in the moment of her ecstasy, but he wanted to feel her pulse over him, wanted to have her contract around his erection inside her. If she needed to keep control herself, then he did not mind - for now. He let go and fell back onto his elbows. His thighs had begun to feel a little uncomfortable with her weight on them, but he did not want to break the mood by suggesting a new position. Theres leant back against the foot of the bed and opened her eyes wide to look at him.

' I will teach you some time, but not today.'

'What do you want me to do?' he inquired. He was hungry for her and keen to know how to please her.

'Just stay there, and I will tell you. You just need to make sure that you stay safely inside, I don't want to hurt you!'

His face flushed as he concentrated hard. His cock became harder than before, as she held him in her secret place. He could feel his own desire rise and knew his own oblivion was not far off, but this was to be her moment. Tom wanted to see her use him. A sense of perversity made him hold his breath. He would let her use him whenever she wanted to, that much was clear.

She leaned back on him, her secret button exposed to her fingers. Her muscles tensed to hold on to the upright soldier deep inside her.

'Is that too tight for you?' she asked, making sure. Tom shook his head. She seemed matter-of-fact, but the gentle flush on her face betrayed her urgency.

Theres moistened the fingertips of her right hand, and began to stroke herself. She had her eyes closed, he watched her face intently. Tom knew that she needed to dis-associate herself from him to reach her climax, but he also had learned that she enjoyed his proximity, his manhood inside her sex, and that it helped her towards her most sensuous heights to know that he was watching her. She looked like she was concentrating for a serious task. He remained quiet within her.

Theres rubbed her clitoris harder and faster. Bright pink infused her cheeks. Her fanny contracted, and her whole weight bore down on him, making sure he would feel her constrict and climax. Her hand moved faster and faster. Suddenly, she moaned shouted 'Yes, yes, now....', voice pitched high, her face contorted as in agony, and her haunches lifted up so that he barely managed to remain within. Her climax swept her away, and her inner secretions flooded him, as she quivered and jerked and her sex pulsed around his prick. One last labored sigh escaped her. Then she laughed hysterically.

'Did you like that?' she asked. Before he could answer, she stood up and declared 'I need another shower!'

CHAPTER 11

Tom's glance fell on Theres as they dressed. Her body glistened from the second shower and emanated freshness. From where he stood, he could smell the faint aroma of her shower gel. The skin of her face was pale and translucent. He longed to touch her but he knew that there was a place and a time for intimacy in their relationship. Now was not it. Her hair curled around her shoulders. He loved it when she left it like that. So natural.

As he watched her, he felt tenderness and yearning, at the same time old like time and new like nothing else ever before. He often wondered whether he could spend the rest of his life with this beautiful young woman; just walk away from life as he had known it, to begin afresh with her.

She took his breath away, and every day was new and exciting. But moments like this made him conscious of his own age. How could he ever hope to keep this woman happy and content? She was so much more to him than any of the others before her. She was inspiration and life, an excellent travelling companion, a wonderful conversationalist, and an intimate friend. He often had dreamt about a woman like her, but had never known one till now. He watched as she now sat on the bed to put on her tights. She had advised him that there was a surprise for him that night, that she had organised an activity away from the other passengers on the train. Intrigued, he wondered what it could be.

So far, they had kept to themselves, hardly interacting with the others, and their absence would not be noted. There had not been the need to be with others. Theres had been enough of a companion, and they always found topics to discuss. When they ran out of words, there was always action. Their minds and their bodies were in tune, so silence only brought them closer. There was no point negating it - he was in love, and he hoped he could get through the turmoil his feelings were bringing. Never seeing her again was too much to bear. Even if he could not leave Lillian, he would find a way to remain close to Theres. She was so important and his life had changed so much since they had known each other. Four months now - and yet, it seemed like an eternity. He could no longer remember what life was like without Theres. Before Theres, there had not been life, only 'getting by'. He now realised that he had done nothing but wait. Waited for his opportunity to meet this woman.

He stood in the middle of their bedroom, watching Theres and at the same time getting dressed himself. Theres became aware that he was looking at her, unmoving, and she glanced up at him. Her smile greeted him joyfully. There was a lacy section at the top of her slip, close where the legs joined, and it looked as though she was wearing stockings. The effect was tempting.

'You okay?' she asked. Tom nodded.

'I was just thinking. About you.'

'Do I need to know what you were thinking?' She stood up and pulled her tights all the way over her thighs and into place.

'I was thinking that if you were mine, I would not force you to have my children.'

'What?' Theres flushed crimson. 'What did you say?'

'If you were mine, I would be content with you. You would be all the family I would ask for, you would be enough.'

'Tom, this is...'

'I know, it is none of my business. At the same time, it grieves me to think that in a few months' time, you go back to the clinic and try again for a baby with a man you don't love. Just to make your marriage work.'

'Tom', she protested, 'this is not why I want a baby.' Her face showed her distaste of his having approached the topic of her childlessness. She had been quite open with him about it, had told him of the two miscarriages she had suffered the previous year and the strain this had put on her relationship with Ben. Tom knew that it was Ben who wanted children. He also was aware that Ben wanted children to make up for the loss of his own when his first marriage ended in divorce. Theres had not said so in so many words, but it seemed obvious.

'I want to try for a baby because sooner rather than later it will be too late. I biologically won't be able to be a mother, and I don't want to wake up in ten years, thinking that I missed out.'

Tears rose in her eyes. Tom had not wanted to upset her, he had hoped to reassure her about their future. He would not force her to undergo any more treatments. It would hurt him to know about more painful injections, operations and disappointment when yet again she would not conceive. She had told him about all this, and he had been grateful for her trust in him. He had been looking for an affair with a younger woman, all those months ago, to maybe start all over again, to have another child, but Theres was more than a link in the biological chain, and suddenly the thought of a new family was no longer important. Only Theres.

'If we were together, would you still want a baby? Mind you, I would not ask you for one.'

Theres shook her head. She sat down on her hands, her legs pulled up close and her feet crossed. She averted her face from him. He so wanted to go and comfort her, but sensed that she would not appreciate his touch now.

'Tom, this hurts.'

He sat down on the bed, not touching, but close.

'I know. I just wanted to tell you, that if we stay together, if there is a 'me and you', an 'us', just you and me will be enough for me. You are going to be my family. I have thought about this ever since you told me about your illness. I even looked it up on the Internet, just so I knew what you were going through and what to expect. There is a chance that one day, you might conceive, even though this chance is smaller than a win in your National Lottery. If you want to be a mother, you don't have to give birth. We could adopt. We'll see how things go. I just would not want you to go through what you went through already. And I hope you don't go back to the clinic with Ben, I would not want to see you stay with him for the sake of a child, that would be wrong, for all three of you. I am giving you an opportunity here, I just want you to know what I feel like.'

He rolled onto the bed and took her hand. Large tears were still falling down her face and he needed to console her. He had made her cry, and he was sorry. But he had needed to say what he did. He had thought about it long enough.

'I want you to know how much I love you and that your illness, your condition, has no influence on my acceptance of you. If you are willing to have me, that is. One day, maybe...'

With the back of her hand, Theres wiped away her tears. There was the beginning of a smile on her face already.

'Are you saying there is going to be a future for us?'

'I am saying we should concentrate on what we have now. The future will develop all by itself. We can try and shape it in our favour, but we should not be disappointed if it works out differently. Come here and let me hug you. I love you, don't you forget that!'

She curled into him and began to relax. Their future lay ahead, just a breath away, always just a breath away.

CHAPTER 12

The evening air hung thick and heavy over the river when they walked the short distance to the landing pier. For a while, they looked at the cruise boats that operated along the Danube all summer long. Eventually, Theres led him onto one, and they paid to be taken north to see the sights from the river.

Tom had always felt at home with rivers, he could never fully explain their deep meaningfulness to anybody. Theres at least tried to understand, and she knew that it would please him to float along the Danube for a while. The atmosphere aboard ship was relaxed, people were chatting excitedly, taking photographs, eating, drinking and laughing together. They enjoyed it, not just for the fact that they were together and care-free.

Theres and Tom listened to a running commentary describing the buildings and bridges on either side. Tom had to laugh - this commentary was in several languages, English being the last, so that by the time he could make out what was said, he had to crane his neck as the building of interest was already past. He pointed this out to Theres and she helped by translating for him the German that came a second after the Hungarian.

'The bridge we are going to see next is the Elizabeth Bridge. When it was built around 1900, it was the longest suspension bridge in the world. It got destroyed in the Second World War, but later rebuilt in its current shape.' The bridge cast a shadow over their boat when they glided under it.

'Right - I don't know about you, but to me, this is a bridge. Don't know what else to say about it', Theres added.

'Well, I am sure the people from Buda and Pest are real proud of it.'

Tom beamed at her. He was happy. They had managed to get seats along a panorama window, and they held hands across the table. He could not be without touching her, he needed to feel her close. Theres never seemed to evade his touch, she seemed to make herself available for his caresses, and made him feel at ease with his own physical need for her. He looked at her and felt this need like a pain rise in his stomach. If only there weren't all these people around them, he would kiss her and show her to what heights of passion he could rise. Instead, he gently tugged at her hands.

'You are good as a tour guide. Are you sure you have never been here before?'

'Well', she admitted, 'I read the travel guide before we started, I just forgot to bring it along.'

They laughed. The warmth between them mingled and rose in the air. Everybody could see how much they cared for one another, how much they were made for each other, and how important was their love.

'This next bridge was built ... I didn't catch that, they are talking German with a strange accent! ... but two English men were involved, both called Clark but not related. It is supported by two towers and ... quite long. Sorry about that, I will try and listen better next time!'

Another bridge went by overhead.

'Apparently, the eastern bank is a little boring as regards architecture. You might be able to see the dome and towers of St Stephen's Basilica. O, look', Theres pointed. 'That must be it!'

Tom did not care for the views outside. He was glad that Theres had made him come, he could go home and read up on all the sights they had seen, but right now, his mind was elsewhere. In his mind, he was working out what to tell Lillian once he got back home, and how he could share his life between these two women without losing them both.

'And that is the parliament. The dome is visible from wherever you are along the Danube in central Budapest. A bit like the Houses of Parliament. Maybe there is something in rivers, that people build places of power along them. Just never thought of that.'

'Rivers always were important for trade and therefore money and wealth. Or the absence of it', Tom threw in absentmindedly. 'As buildings go, these aren't bad. I have to admit I am not all that knowledgeable about architecture. But I like to see it. And you can teach me to appreciate it better!'

Theres grinned. 'Only from the guidebook. I think I could tell you about Art Nouveaux, but that is about all I know about architecture. But isn't this nice? Look, there is a family of ducks!'

For a short while, they watched the birds float along in the wake of the boat. They had nearly reached the northernmost part of their trip, and now tuckered their way around Margaret Island. Tom made a mental note to maybe go and visit the landscaped gardens the next morning. But then, Theres might have made other plans.

'See this island?' She piped. 'There were Dominican nuns on there in the thirteenth century. King Bela's daughter Margaret came to live there and that is why it is called Margaret's Island. Before then, it was called Rabbits' Island. I read about it and was somehow taken with its story, so I remembered. Nowadays, there are walks all across the island, and there is a swimming pool and other sports facilities. Like a green lung in the middle of Budapest.'

At the table next to them, a family with several children had settled into a noisy picnic. A little girl now approached Theres and tugged timidly at her sleeves. When Theres faced her, the girl smiled and held out some bread and sausage. For a moment, Theres was stunned. Then, she turned towards the rest of the family and nodded acceptance.

'Köszönöm', Theres said and their new friends roared with happy laughter. The man and woman were in their forties, well-nourished and happy. Two of the girls wore traditional dress. Thick yellow pleats of hair framed their shiny pink faces. The bread was fresh and the sausage tasty.

'Do you have something to share?' Theres asked. 'This is so nice of them! Strangers sharing their food with us, I would like to give them something in return!'

Tom looked around. From a small bar, an old man sold drinks. 'I am sure, Father would not mind a drink, he looks that kind of chap. What do the Hungarians drink? Slivovic?' he was not sure, but as always relied on Theres.

'See whether they do Palinka. That is some sort of fruit brandy. And get one for mother, too, she looks that way as well!' Theres giggled.

Tom got up and went to the bar. While he ordered the drinks, Theres turned to face the family again and they smiled at each other. Father nodded and asked 'American?' to which Theres pointed at Tom and said 'American'. Then, she pointed at herself and said 'English'. Both the man and woman nodded, all the while smiling at her.

The woman asked something else of her that Theres did not understand. She shook her head and shrugged her shoulders. The woman pointed to her left hand and Theres looked down. Her wedding band and engagement ring were showing. She raised her hand and twirled the rings. The woman nodded and pointed to Tom. She must think them married. Theres replied with happy nodding. After all, she and Tom were married - just not to each other. That was hard to explain in a foreign language and on a cruise along the Danube.

In turn, she pointed at the five children - three boys and two girls and signed her question as to whether they all belonged to the man and woman. Their smiles changed in intensity and became proud and even happier. They introduced their brood - Gregor, Ferenc and Paul; Gretha and Elspeth (the little girl that had offered her the food earlier), and all were made to parade in front of her. The boys bowed politely and the girls curtsied shyly. Father turned out to be Ferenc senior, and Mother was Marie. Theres introduced herself and Tom.

When he returned to the table, Theres had joined the others. Forgotten were the sights along the riverbanks, important cultural exchange took place. Tom had brought glasses with plum brandy (szilva palinka) for the adults, and lemonade for the children. All was accepted with gratitude, more bread and sausage came out, the talk around the table became louder and more raucous. They laughed at each other, and then Theres drew a map of their journey so far. Ferenc and Marie and the children were impressed, as far as Tom could make out, as this trip to their capital had been the furthest they had ever come. There was pointing at the children, and the rubbing together of fingers - a flock of five little ones could not be combined with international travel. But they had seen America on the TV, and they knew all about it.

Ferenc senior stroked his moustache and barked 'I'll be back', laughed and nodded 'Arnold, Arnold'. They laughed.

Later, Tom and Theres could only vaguely remember the view of the Castle, or any of the churches along the western bank. They went under several more bridges, but their time was taken up with their new companions. Little Gretha had taken a shine to Theres, and cradled herself into her lap. They seemed to be utterly at ease. Theres held on to the girl, and together they were talking in a language that consisted of pointing and showing, drawing and a lot of laughter. It touched Tom deeply to see Theres this happy and relaxed. Gretha was five years old, two years younger than her sister, and seemed a happy child. They all were. They all seemed to be healthy, well fed and the archetypal Slavic family. Ferenc and Gregor showed Tom their new books, picture books of Budapest, telling of the city's history.

'Tom?' Theres interrupted his concentration on the boys.

'Yes, dear?' She looked at him intently and he knew that she had an idea.

'Could we go and have dinner with these people? I am sure they can take us somewhere Hungarian ... would you mind?'

He looked up from the books and saw her mind ticking away, making plans, fermenting.

'If you can get them to understand what you are after, then I won't mind. They are nice enough. As long as they are not coming with us back to the hotel or anything. I would hate having to share you any longer than necessary.' His eyes twinkled impishly at that last comment.

Theres pushed Gretha off her lap and looked around. One of the stewards seemed to have been able to understand a little English. She approached him and asked his help in translating for her.

'Please, can you ask them whether they would come to dinner with us? We would like them to take us somewhere Hungarian, where we could eat Hungarian food, just like they would. We invite them, tell them we pay. Please?'

The man thought for a brief second, not certain that he had completely understood. Then, he launched into a language that Theres had no way of understanding. She and Tom could only hope that their interpreter did as she had asked him. After to-ing and fro-ing, their outing was agreed, and they got off at the next pier.

With children skipping around them like a breath of fresh air, they made their way into Central Pest, and entered a tiny restaurant. The simple interior was decked with white walls and white kitchen tables. On the walls hung photographs of famous Hungarians, of whom neither Theres nor Tom could recognise anyone. They waited before a table got free that was large enough to hold all nine of them. Even then, it was a squeeze. Gretha had managed to catch the seat right next to Theres. Marie looked on as her younger daughter made conversation with the strange foreign lady. Marie did not mind.

Ferenc Senior ordered. Tom was overwhelmed when their meal arrived. The waiter presented small plates of different meats, stuffed peppers, and, most importantly, fresh bread. Ceremoniously, he brought two bottles of white, crisp Hungarian wine. He sat opposite Theres and he watched her with the child. He knew what he had told her about being a biological mother, but he suddenly could see that her nature was caring and supportive of a child's whims. She would make a natural mother, one day, and he suddenly felt deeply sorry and grieved that his Theres should be denied the pleasure of motherhood.

The children quietened down, and conversation turned into grunts of approval. After the haute cuisine of the Orient Express, Tom did not really need this grand banquet, but the food was delicious and festive. They ate with their fingers. Fat dripped off faces. Sauce got splashed. He loved this time, this place, these people. He loved her.

As plates emptied, and contentedness descended upon the group, Marie pointed again. 'Édességek?'

Theres beamed. 'Tom, that one I know! Trust me!'

To Marie she said 'Igen. Palacsinta.'

She smiled. Gretha obviously approved of whatever Theres had said. Ferenc called out to a waiter and ordered something new. The other children cheered as well.

'Have you ordered ice cream or something?'

A short nod from Theres and a gleam in her eyes confirmed his assessment of the situation.

'Dessert. A Hungarian speciality, just wait and see.'

He would never be able to grasp how she knew all these things, he would ask her about the food some time, and about her understanding of all those languages. He managed to get by in English, and he had his American tongue. But Theres was fluent in German, spoke passable French, and now communicated with Hungarians in a way that they understood. She always surprised him, as beauty never fails to surprise a man with eyes to see.

'Palacsinta' turned out to be pancakes, almond filled and flambéed for the adults, and filled with jam for the children. Heavy, dark chocolate accompanied the desert, adding to the multitude of flavours and educating Tom's taste buds. The children ate in silence.

When the meal was over and Theres asked for the bill, Ferenc and Marie tried to argue over the paying, but Theres understood unerringly that it was only a token argument, and would not have them share what was an insignificantly small amount for herself and Tom - given that a meal for two in their hotel would have cost more than they spent in the small restaurant amongst nine contented patrons.

Good-byes were said, and Gretha cried. She did not want to let go of Theres. Marie had to drag her away and Ferenc carried her a while, talking at her and trying to calm her. Gregor had a small camera, and Theres had to pose with Gretha before the girl would stop crying. Gretha would have a photo to remember Theres by. Tom wished he could have this photograph, but he could not return home with such a souvenir. All he could do was memorise the scene and hoping he would never forget.

They walked back, hand in hand, towards the Danube and hoped that they would be able to find their hotel. Theres felt light and happy, it had been a wonderful day. Tom put his arm around her and held her close.

'You are wonderful, do you know that?' Fear was about to overwhelm him. He needed her close, and he needed to feel her there by his side. He needed her assurance that the time together would be enough to last them a lifetime.

'And I love you. For being generous and letting me take control like this. I am turning into a right little general, and it is giving me pleasure. Because I can see that you like it, too. Like tonight, taking Ferenc and Marie out. I love you for that!'

Her eyes clouded over, he saw the depth of her emotions. Theres, his Theres. He kissed her.

'And I love you!'

'And what is tomorrow going to bring?' he wanted to know.

'We can talk about that. Later.'

They walked on.

'Theres, what is on your mind? Tell me, I want to know!'

Theres sighed. How could she explain?

'There is nothing, really. Just that I enjoyed being with those children. I liked little Gretha. And maybe, just maybe, it hurts to think that there never will be a little Gretha of my own. One, that I made, that is part of me. But this thought will go, and I am still here with you, and that makes me happier than anything else ever. And nobody can take that from me. If I want to remember anything from today, it is the nice new friends we made. Do you know that they think we are married? Marie asked me and I couldn't tell her different...'

'Is that a problem? I mean, that people think us married?'

'Of course not! But I would have thought that we are too much in love to be thought of as a married couple!' She laughed and skipped off his hand. Numbered boxes were chalked on the pavement. They had faded numbers in them. Rain would soon wash it all away, but for now some child's entertainment invited Theres to express her own contented happiness.

'We used to play this at school', she said pointing to the ground.

Tom had not noticed before. Now, he skipped after her, like a young boy, this man of late middle age.

'We did that, too', he said, 'Hopscotch', and they laughed. They had reached the Danube, and they could see their hotel across Szabadsag Bridge. Hand in hand, they ran across and fell into each other's arms.

CHAPTER 13

Their hotel was renowned for its baths complex. So, the next morning, Theres and Tom sauntered out to sample the wave pool towards the back of the complex. Even though this part of the baths had been built in the late 1920s, the mechanism still functioned. At nine o'clock, the day promised to be summery, and the cool water refreshing.

Tom saw Theres in a swimsuit for the first time, black and high-cut, showing off strong, shapely thighs. It fitted snuggly, zipped up in the back, a proper swimmer's outfit. When he had asked about it, she laughed. 'You know, anything else and I would fall out', she had joked, and he could believe her. Her breasts were magnificent, above average in size and in need of a strong hold. He knew that she showed her nakedness generously to him, but she made a point of hiding her assets from others. She hated -especially -- men who talked to her chest. He could understand a man's visual response, and her breasts were inviting ...

Swimming trunks had not been on her list of things to bring, but he had packed some shorts that would do. Next to her, he felt conscious of his body. She had never said, but he could do with looking after his bulk. Then he remembered that Ferenc and Marie had thought them a married couple. They had seen them as 'together', and that calmed him a little. He just hoped that the whole world would realize they were truly together, that they belonged together and would forever remain so.

'You know', she now said, 'that the others from the train are meeting at 12:00 for lunch? I told the tour guide that we would be there, a taxi will call for us at 11:30. We have to be ready by then!'

'We can stay in here for two hours, if you like'.

The wave machine kicked in every fifteen minutes, stirring the water into movement, like the real ocean, but without the force and more controlled. Neither was the water salty. A good imitation. Theres loved the ocean, she had described the waves crashing into the beach at Aberdeen, the frothing of the Sea on a stormy, heady day. He could see her standing on a wind-swept shore, her hair being blown about and framing her face. He could see and feel her intensity. There was something female about the Ocean, something strong and powerful like only Woman could be. She, too, was powerful. He could feel it and it made him humble. She was so special, so natural. And for now, so utterly 'his'.

'I have a better idea. Come with me!'

She pulled herself out of the water and waited for Tom to follow. Then, shivering and dripping puddles, she walked over to another pool, smaller with rising steam.

'You see, this is the hot pool, and it has medicinal spa water. I am not quite sure what makes it medicinal, I am just glad it doesn't smell too bad of rotten eggs. Let us see what it does for us!'

The water was indeed hot, and sheltered from the view of the summer terrace. No other patrons were around. Theres went in first and gasped when she immersed herself.

'This is fine, this is!' she exclaimed. 'Come on!'

Theres swam to the center of the pool and waited for Tom. When he reached her, she slung her arms around him. They stood on their toes and they embraced.

'Are you happy, my wonderful Tom?' she nestled her head against his ear. Her body was close. The water supported her weight, as her legs enfolded his waist. He held her there.

'I wish we were entirely alone, and nobody could walk in on us', he whispered.

'I know', she replied. His erection pressed against her, and impressed on her his need. 'But right now, there is nobody here but us.'

'Theres, I couldn't...' Tom was aghast.

'Why not? There is just a little bit of cloth needing moved, and nobody would see.' Her hand went down between their bodies. She shifted his shorts a little, and when she moved her own gusset, he slid right into her. Tom gasped.

'Theres...!' but his need was too great for him to stop. He held her in his arms, impaled on his erection, and kissed her with new intensity. The danger of being found out added a distinct level of excitement, in the middle of the hot pool, making love for all to see. When Theres kissed him, he pushed his tongue in between her lips and greedily licked and sucked.

Theres tilted her hips and moved his erection within her. He slowly bounced with the motion of the water, balancing her, feeling her weight shift slightly, swaying with the movement of their union. The heat increased their passion and before long, Tom erupted within her. Theres stifled his sound with her mouth. She glided back onto her own feet and held him close.

'Theres ... I have never done this! My God, that was ... that was...' and words failed him. He stood and held her.

'I have never done this either. Are you sorry we did?'

'No! No, but this was ... O, Theres, my Theres! Don't forget, I am of a more conservative make then you are. Making love to you here, in public ... Theres!'

He kissed her again and again. When people approached the little hot pool, they had to let go of each other. Tom straightened his shorts and made sure he was not showing. Theres pulled her swimsuit into place, and they left, too overpowered to speak.

CHAPTER 14

The Orient Express headed south and east in almost a straight line from Budapest to Bucharest. Rural Hungary passed before their eyes, swathed in the sun of a summer afternoon. Fields and pasture stretched for as far as their eyes roamed. Often, a small village loomed at the edge of their vision. The land seemed empty and forlorn.

'This is not what I expected', Tom offered.

'What did you expect?' Theres was keen to talk.

'Men on horses for one. You know, they have their own brand of cowboys here, but they are not called that. And more cattle.' He looked at her. 'You know I am a romantic at heart. The great Austro-Hungarian Empire and all that. Sissy, the child-like empress. To be truthful, I was a little disappointed that there was nobody playing the fiddle in the restaurant last night - or at lunch today, for that matter!'

'I am glad there were no fiddles in the restaurant last night - there would not have been enough room! I would have been really embarrassed if there had been musicians coming to the table I was at, so I sure didn't hope for that kind of attention!'

'As for cowboys, I know what you mean. Hungarians are famed for their horsemanship. They are called czikós, I think. Not sure. I don't know whether they are not just in a particular part of the country, rather than anywhere. Like the puszta. Do you call that 'steppe'? I honestly don't know!'

'Have you ever traveled around here? Didn't you say your family was from somewhere 'Slavic'?'

Theres sighed. They had journeyed through Hungary once, a long time ago, and into Yugoslavia, when she was about six or seven. It had been Christmas, when the communist rule had not allowed Christmas to be celebrated as a Christian festival any longer. Hungary had been extremely poor and she remembered the wells, the forlorn wells, rising all along the horizon, where horsemen and cattle found refreshment. Primitive shelters against the wind. Watered down petrol finished off the engine of their car. They left it behind, and fetched it over New Year, on the back of a hired van whose driver had known of a way through the passes, beyond border control, and her mother and she had found refuge in a hotel. There had been strange noises through the thin walls, and she had been intrigued by why rooms should have been paid for by the hour. Her mother had locked and bolted the door, they had lived off a few groceries and bottled juices for a day or two, till the men came back with the car.

But she didn't want to tell Tom all this. These were not happy memories, they were of a time that bore no happy recollections for her. She did not want to explain to him just then.

'No, not really', she eventually volunteered. 'Not that I can remember, anyway. And I never went back to see where my grandparents were from. They did, though. The house of Grandma's family was still there, still used as a farm. I think they were quite relieved about that. Relieved and happy, because the family who had the farm were looking after it well.'

'You love your Grandparents, don't you?'

'So would you if you had been in my shoes! They were always there for me, and they still are. I dread the day when one of them dies and I am left without them. Both of them. I don't know how I will cope, and I hope it is a long time hence!'

He knew that her thoughts made her sad, but there had not been sadness when she spoke, just a melancholy that he suddenly had the urge to wipe away.

'Tell me about them, where they are from!'

'If you like.' She thought and wondered for a moment about what would make him happy to hear about her origin.

'My family is German as long as anybody can remember. You know, in the Thirties, that was an important thing to prove. True Aryans. German through and through. Blond and blue-eyed. Good stock. A few hundred years back, I reckon, my family were poor farmers. Second sons that didn't inherit, daughters too ugly to marry well ... that type of thing.' She chuckled. 'The Austro-Hungarians had this bit of land that they had taken over and that was populated by a people that wasn't too happy about their new rulers. So, they agreed with the Germans that poor German folk would get land to farm there, make and keep peace with the locals and all the way being governed by the Germans. Win-win for all around -apart from the indigenous folk. My Grandparents call them 'Boschnaks' which makes me believe they are Bosnians.'

'Anyway, my ancestors were part of that poor populace that got some land there. They all had a house, some gardens around them and some fields outside the village. I think my great-grandfather's plot had a well. There was a communal baking house and a church and a school. Two schools, really. That is, a German school and a 'boschnak' school. By the time my grandparents were little, Grandma's father was the most important man in the village, and the richest. He was the mayor. They had horses and vineyards and hired hands to do their dirty work. They worked hard, but then people in those days always seemed to.

'Granddad's family on the contrary were very poor.

'Granddad himself was a swineherd when he was a boy, and he only got permission to marry my grandmother as a baby was on the way. My oldest uncle. And then the war came, Germany could no longer support and protect their enclaves and called all good Germans back into the Reich. My family lost everything, and just went and started all over.'

Tom listened, fascinated. It always amazed him that Theres could talk about history as though she had been there. She had a keen interest in her family's story, and she had spent more time with her great-grandparents and the other old folk than most youngsters. She had told him how much she had loved her grandmother's mother and how she hurt when the old woman died. He could sit and listen to her for hours, imagining that he knew the places and people she spoke of. He knew her heart was with all those whose story she so eloquently brought to life for him.

'What would your grandparents say if they knew about us?' he suddenly inquired of her. This thought had weighed on his heart for some time, as he was aware that their approval would mean more to Theres than anybody else's.

'Why do you ask? Does it matter to you whether they would approve of you - of us?'

'I think it would matter to you. And I wondered. They must have been married for many years now, so I think that would make them want to see you stay with Ben. No?'

'They celebrated their 60th anniversary last year. But they have seen their children divorced - my oldest uncle is currently on his fourth wife, my second uncle is still married to the same woman even though they haven't slept together for quite a while, and my mother is married for the third time. And she had a whole set of boyfriends in-between. They like Ben, but they love me. If I chose to be with somebody else, they would always give them the benefit of the doubt. They would always invite them into their fold with open arms. If you and I got together, we would spend most of our life in the States, so they would not see all that much of either of us. No matter what - they would love and accept you because I love you, it is as easy as that.'

'Is it?'

'They would not judge either of us for our love.'

'Don't they love Ben?'

'They do, but only as long as he is with me. As long as he is with me, they treat him as one of their own. I am sure they would always remember him fondly, but they would never make me stay with him. Do you think your daughter, Jenny, would mind about me?'

Tom grappled for breath. 'You know, I don't even want to think about that. I can see her get really angry at you if she knew about us. She probably would hate both you and me and never speak to me again.' He fell silent. The thought of losing the easy confidence he had with his daughter weighed heavily. Also the loss of Megan made his decision about a future with Theres so difficult. He wished he could sustain both Lillian and Theres, and keep them apart and secret from each other. He also understood that this was not fair to either.

Theres studied him for a moment before continuing along a different line of thought.

'They are dark thoughts, let us banish them. Let us enjoy the time we have together, the future we can dream about and think of later, it will come all by itself and then we see. How about going to the bar car and listen to the piano for a while? Somehow I think I could do with a little drink. And then, we can watch the sun set over Hungary and curl up together.'

When they left their compartment, Tom whispered into her hair and at first she could not hear what it was. He had to repeat:

'Was your grandmother really pregnant before she married?'

Theres had to stifle a laugh. She turned to face him and looked deep into his eyes. Her face twinkled all over and it was hard not to burst out laughing.

'Are you worried about the morality of my family? Well, six months after Grandma married, she gave birth to a healthy, large bouncing baby boy. Nobody could have believed he was three months premature.'

Together, arm in arm, they strolled into the bar car, laughing. He loved her and he would forever love her family and all about them. Even their loose morality. Particularly, if it allowed for making love the way they did!

CHAPTER 15

That night, they decided to sleep in the same single bed. It was tight, but they were close together. Togetherness had become important. Neither could be without the other for long.

Theres wore pajamas during the night, and insisted keeping her uppers so that her shoulders would not get cold. Tom discarded his usual nightly shorts and bedded down next to her, naked. The proximity was delicious. They rested against each other, relishing their warmth.

They chattered away over the day's events and their feelings, about what they had seen and experienced. They did not speak of their love or future. That night, their focus was on the tangible and present-past. Talk ambled along, and sleep was ages away. Sleep never came easy when they were together.

As before, Theres rested her head on Tom's chest, close to his heart. With one hand supporting her neck, his other began to stroke her naked leg resting easily on his. In response, Theres caressed his face. Theres slipped off her top and her generous breasts nestled against his ribcage.

He turned and kissed her. The first coming together of their lips was gentle and playful, the second more passionate. His wandering hand moved in between her thighs, found the moistness of her pleasure, stroked, probed and titillated her into small whimpers. When Theres' breath came in gasps and her body shuddered with silent excitement, his fingers kissed her silken, hidden pearl, and he pulled her across him, his hand all the while keeping hold of her love. Theres straddled him, having to rest one foot on the cold floor, and took him in slowly and delicately. Their lips became fixed, and their tongues relentlessly probed and explored.

Theres pushed herself up, supporting her weight on her hands on either side of his head. Tom sucked in a nipple in front of his eyes.

His hand still rubbed Theres, and she demanded him to stop.

'Just hold it there', she whispered, her face like in a dream, flushed, eyes clouded over. Tom always thought her beautiful, but never more so than in these moments when their love united them as man and woman.

He watched her, his loins hurting for her passion, his hand against her clit. She was breathtaking. Their sex was breathtaking. It was not the mainstay of their relationship, but nevertheless, it always was there with its excitement and excellence. Her body was ambrosia for his masculinity. He had to look at her, see her perform the most mundane tasks and he wanted her desperately. His body reacted to her like he had never thought possible. It had been a long time since he had made love to anybody like they were making love together now. Never had Woman been more exciting and new.

She had closed her eyes, her face concentrated in an intensity of pleasure. Her features had become ageless, the little fine lines around her eyes erased. Tenderness, and an immense need to protect and love her, flooded through Tom, and made him shift inside her. His gentle motion made her react, and her hips began to tilt back and forth in an ever-increasing build-up, till the rhythm reached its crescendo, as the train thundered eastward into the night.

Tom could not hold back and his seed erupted, flooding her and filling her. Theres opened her eyes wide, not seeing, her head spinning to and fro, hair flailing. She held on to him inside her, her body convulsed violently above him, engulfing him in her fire, before exhausting her crisis with one last bout of furious movement that took his breath, and alarmed him at the same time.

She fell onto Tom, holding him so close that he feared suffocation. The heat of their bodies mingled with the cooling air till very much later, his erection crumpled and slipped out, sheathed in their moistness, and leaving stains on the clean new sheets.

CHAPTER 16

'Do you think these croissants are really fresh?'

'I don't know, Tom, I wouldn't have thought so. It takes hours to make them fresh, and I can't see them do that when they can buy croissants and just bake them up before serving them.'

They enjoyed a quiet breakfast in their compartment. Outside, the early morning haze shrouded the sun and lingered longer than they had expected. Already, fiery air encroached through the slightly lowered window.

'I think we should ask the valet for some garlic.' Theres offered mischievously.

'Garlic?' Tom could at the moment not make the connection. 'I thought you were not allowed garlic, it made you ill?'

'O', she exclaimed. 'Not for me, my love! Garlic to fend off the vampires! You know there are some that can survive in the daylight ... and this IS Transylvania after all!' She laughed happily. He fell in with her.

'To be honest, Theres, I don't know much about vampires.' Her mood was catching.

'But they live around here. Or at least, this is where they originally come from. Do you know the writing of Pratchett, Terry Pratchett?'

Tom shook his head. She enlightened, charmed, educated and brought her own world and spin closer to him. And spinning he was, light-headed! His world had become a dream, the dream that Theres wove for him.

'He writes about Disc World. Disc World is flat, and carried through Universe on the back of four giant elephants which stand on the back of A-tuin, the great turtle. There are several continents on disc world, and there is a region called Uberwald. Which, if you think of it, translates kind of into Transylvania. This region is dark and mysterious and is populated by ... let me think ... dwarfs that live below it. They do the mining, and there is a lot of gold involved. There are the 'Igors' who all talk with a lisp and are good at sewing. They are made of body parts and when one of them passes away, his parts are donated to others. They are stitched together by hand. I identify with that, I like sewing, too.'

She looked at him to gauge his interest. His eyes told her that he was listening intently, so she continued.

'There are all sorts there, but most importantly there are werewolves and vampires. Vampires tend to be quite bright and intelligent, so when they realized that they only could survive as a race if they conformed, they had to stop sucking blood to get on in life. When they leave Uberwald and move to Ankh Morpok, which is a major town, they join this 'club' which is very much like the AA. They have meetings and they sing, and they abstain from the 'b-word'. For their efforts, they get this little blue medal to hold on to in times when their urge gets too much to control. I also tried to read 'Dracula', but I think I was too young and didn't quite get it.'

'Tell me more', Tom pleaded when she suddenly fell silent.

'There is nothing more to tell.'

'Why do you then call one of your colleagues 'the vampire'? Does he have a little blue medal?' His voice was mocking her, but kindly.

'You remember that, do you?' She smiled and thought a little. Tom held her gaze.

'You see, there are times when a teetotal vampire sees the neck of a young maiden, all white and pure. His urge to suck returns...'

'I know this urge', he interrupted huskily.

'His urge returns', she ignored him, 'and if he is not careful, he will give in...'

'I want to give in to my urge', he interrupted again.

'Tom', she sounded like a schoolmistress. 'Do you want me to tell you or not?'

'Yes, dear. I want you. Naked. Right in front of me, so I can touch you and devour you, my young and pure maiden.'

Theres shook her head. 'You know, a week ago, you would not have spoken to me like this!'

'A week ago I had not tasted your love. You have changed me. You have made me experience pleasure like I had never felt it before. I am your slave, I live by your love.'

His voice expressed an urgency and a truth that Theres was not prepared for that morning. They had spent the whole night closely intertwined in his bed, enwrapped and sheltered in each other's arms. The morning had come and they had broken away from each other when their passion rekindled and he had entered her once more, with a tenacity and seriousness she had not felt in him before. When he withdrew, his seed had not been spilt but his thirst had been quenched for the instant. The scene had left her strangely touched.

Their love had grown, evolved and changed. It was sincere and terribly needy. At times, this need overpowered, but never did it oppress.

'I love you, my brave, my wonderful Tom.' Theres stretched out her hand and touched his face, running her fingers gently about his brow and down his nose. When she reached his lips, he gently opened for her and sucked her in. She withdrew.

'We will be in Sinaia soon.'

Tom sat up straight. She was right, he was behaving like a lovesick teenager, not like a man approaching his sixties. There always was the night, later, and they would be together intimately once again. He could wait till then.

'What is so special about Sinaia then?' He was eager for a continuation of his lessons.

'It is apparently an extremely picturesque place. A bit like the Monte Carlo of Rumania, there are casinos and things, where the rich and famous used to gamble. There is skiing, bob sleighing and all sorts of winter sports, and in summer, I suppose, you can walk in the forests. The other thing I remember is the 'health cures', but I am not sure whether that has to with the water or whether it is the air.'

She stood and closed the window.

'So the vampires can't fly in', she said, before she resumed.

'Remember when we were talking about the Bavarians and the Swabians? When I was telling you about their history and I said that the Bavarians always seemed to have been noisier when it came to getting in with royalty?'

Tom nodded. That had been the time when she told him about her bad experiences with the Bavarians and he had marveled at her description of the German races.

'You know that Germany is divided into federal states. My mother lives in Baden Wuerttemberg - I think it is the same in English. Their capital is Stuttgart. Nothing spectacular about Stuttgart apart from the Mercedes Benz factory in the outskirts. But they also have districts and mum's district town is a place called Sigmaringen. That is where the house of Hohenzollern-Sigmaringen come from. One of their lot became King Carol I of Romania in the later half of the 19th century. So, there are Swabians who were involved in monarchy. I was wrong, I admit it!'

'You were wrong, you admit it, but you are still not impressed with the Swabians!' he mocked her.

'You know I am not a Swabian by birth, I just happened to grow up there. Rural Swabia (and there is not much of an industrial Swabia) is a strange place. My mum has lived in the same village for fifteen or more years now, educated their children, but she still is an outsider, and she will remain that. I doubt that they would allow her to be buried there!'

'Do I sense some bitterness?'

'No, no, I don't think so. It's just that I was never really happy there, so when I decided to leave and go to England, it was easy to leave.'

'Surely there must be people you miss? You can't have gone through your teenage years without any friends at all?'

Theres tilted her head and looked at him.

'Are you wondering whether I was not quite normal?' She smiled. Tom returned her gaze openly and without comment.

'Maybe I wasn't. I never had many friends. Those that I call my friends have remained with me. There is one girl that was in my A-level class, and we still are friends. We write, we speak on the phone, we visit each other. I left school sixteen years ago. She still is a friend. Then there is Andy.'

'One of your boyfriends?'

That made her laugh, and it was so infectious that Tom had to join in without knowing why.

'If you ever met Andy you would know better! Andy is the big brother I never had. He is from the village where mum lives, but I only met him after I had left. He is just wonderful and every time I return, I go and visit him, and he gives me these really massive bear hugs, and then we sit and talk, or go out together for the evening, and it is as though we never had been apart. Andy is close to my heart, no matter what people think of him!'

Tom felt a twinge in his chest. Did she speak to her friends about him in words like these? It took him a moment to comprehend his pain as jealousy.

'What do people think of him?'

'Andy is different and does not fit in somehow.'

'Different?'

'Yes. He had an accident when he was nineteen, he nearly did not survive and was in a coma for several months. He is tall and built like a house, but one of his legs is crippled and quite a bit shorter than the other. He also has this large scar just below his Adam's apple. Basically, he is not concerned what people think of him, even if that means he is lonely sometimes. A lot of folk in the village think he lives off his father who owned the local butcher's but who took early retirement when Andy could no longer work as a butcher himself. But Andy does work part-time, and he gets an invalidity pension. Then there are his horses. He has this piece of land, he calls it his 'Ranch', tucked away from the core of the village. He has several horses and ponies and he is forever pottering about, building new sheds and things. In the summer, he takes people around in his carriages. He is just a wonderful person, and a really dear friend.'

Cooling forests passed by outside, unobserved.

'And you never fancied him as more than a friend?' Tom needed to know. Acutely aware of the chronological difference between them, he relished the perverse pain when he made her aware that there might be other men for her one day.

'I sometimes wonder whether I would have left if I had known him before, and at one time, when my first marriage failed, Mum hoped I would return and she encouraged me to spend more and more time with Andy. I think she was convinced that if I fell in love with him, I would stay. As I said - he is like a big brother, nothing more and nothing less!'

She smiled at Tom reassuringly.

'I wish that one day you could meet him. I am not sure what you would think of each other, he is so unrefined, and not at all like you. I know you would try and see past his rough exterior though. As I know he would accept you as being my love.'

'Am I? Your love?' He desired to hear her say it, needed the reassurance and the certainty in her voice when she told him that she loved him and wanted to be with him. He needed her. More and more.

'You know you are.'

'Then tell me!' he urged her.

Theres studied his face. In his eyes she could make out his urgency and the passion he felt for her; and, for an instant, she was frightened of the intensity of his neediness. She had thought him so much stronger, and could not understand the changes their togetherness had brought over him. At the same time, she had begun to hate the notion of ever being without him again. In her mind she had become certain that she was the stronger, the one more in tune with their reality. She had to protect him from his resurgence of spirit and physicality. They both had too much to lose by impatience. If there was to be a future, it had to be well thought-out and carefully constructed.

The train moved deeper into the horseshoe of the Carpathian Mountains. The magnificence of Sinaia loomed and they emerged into the bustle of a market town on a late Monday morning.

CHAPTER 17

The brightness of the day hurt Theres' eyes and she hid behind extra dark shades. Tom watched her intently. There had been a subtle change in her and he yearned to find out what was on her mind. For the moment though, they were stuck with the other passengers on a guided tour around Sinaia and Peles Castle.

Theres had been right, the town was picturesque and around every corner, new views amazed, and the 'oohs' and 'aahs' of their fellow travelers rang through their coach, winding through the roads and alleys, further up the mountain and towards Peles.

Tom did not catch most of the commentary, he looked at Theres by his side. He sat next to her, leaning over her for a better view, as she occupied the window seat. He took her hands in his, and although they touched, he felt her far away. When he kissed her face, she did not respond.

'You okay?' he whispered, concerned for her well being, but Theres only nodded and turned her face away from him.

The coach slowed down outside the castle and the group emerged.

'Hi there', an American voice crooned from behind. 'You must be the lovebirds from first class, we haven't seen you in ages! How are you?'

A woman in a light blue suit, heavy sunglasses and a fancy straw hat stood behind them. Instantly, Theres recognized the woman who had collided with her at the station in Paris, spilling the contents of her handbag.

'How did you like Budapest? Wasn't that place just adorable? And all those pretty people, o, I just loved it! I am going to go back, I promised it to myself!'

Theres looked at Tom, who shrugged. Theres pulled her shades down and focused at the stranger over the top of the rim.

'Yes, we quite liked Budapest', she volunteered, but her eyes hoped to stop the intrusion. The American woman ignored the steely stare. Tom had to bite his lip to suppress a giggle. There he was, in the middle of Romania, about to enter a fairy tale castle, and he watched and compared two women. The contrast of the gregarious and noisy American to his Theres made her the more appealing and natural. Secretly, he squeezed her hand and shot her a twinkle.

'I am Cecily, by the way. So glad I ran into you...'

'You already did that once before', Theres interrupted.

Cecily looked at her inquisitively, so Theres offered:

'Paris? Gare de l'Est?'

'O yes!' The woman recollected the brief scene and explained: 'I was all in a jiffy! Thought I would miss the Express and didn't realize it was just sitting there for a few more hours! Never mind!' She laughed a short and shrill laugh. 'I am dying to find out what first class looks like, but I didn't just want to intrude. Would you mind if I had a peek later on?'

Theres coughed.

'What a pleasure to meet you properly, Cecily. I am Theres, and this is Tom.'

Cecily hooked herself in between them and pushed them along towards the entrance to the Hall.

'You know, I just love the Orient Express. I have read this enchanting novel about it, and I simply had to take a trip. If I had known there was a first class, I would naturally have tried to book that, but my cabin is quite neat and more than plenty for me. I am a widow, you see, and I travel by myself mostly. O, it is so good to meet you two! Where are you from?'

Cecily's exuberance overflowed. Theres felt her a little too much, her patience beginning to reach its limits. Tom thought of ways to get rid of the intruder politely. While Cecily barraged them with chatter, other folk wandered past, smiling as though to say, 'Rather you than me'. In Tom ripened the suspicion that they had not been the first taken over by the expansive Cecily.

'I am from Cleveland, Ohio, myself. I have lived there all my life, but I have traveled everywhere. When my Rupert died, he left me with quite a nest egg, and I don't have to really worry, so I just go where the mood takes me. But tell me about yourselves?'

'Cecily, I am pleased to meet you and all that, but can't you see that you are encroaching on a private conversation? We really would like to be by ourselves, and to be perfectly honest, I for one am not interested in the story of your life!'

Theres' outburst had come as a surprise. Tom had not seen her this angry before. He had never seen her this direct and openly aggressive. Cecily stood with her mouth wide open.

Theres freed herself from the other woman, turned and walked away. Tom stood in stunned wonder and then ran after her. When he caught up with her, he held her close, silently, and watched her shoulders heave and tremble from her tears. People hurried past, embarrassed by the scene.

'O, my love, what is it? You have been upset for a while! Won't you tell me?'

And she turned and clung to him and held him and cried and tried to speak, but words did not come. He held her, and comforted her, and when she was ready to speak, he listened.

'I don't want our journey to end. I want to be with you forever, I don't want you to go back without me, and yet I know you have to. I love you so much! I was trying so hard not to show you that I was upset, and then this woman appeared and babbled away, I just could not hold back. Tom, I am so sorry!'

'Don't be!' His arms held her and he kissed away her tears. When her body stopped quivering and she regained control, they slowly walked back to the coach, hugging each other close and not letting go.

CHAPTER 18

'You are missing out on the castle.'

They were alone in the coach, the others not yet back from their sightseeing. The driver had still been there and was kind enough to let them stay in the coach, while he himself went for a break and most likely for a drink in some local bar.

'I don't miss out on anything. I am with you.' Through her tears, Theres smiled. She had turned from a resourceful, energetic woman into a frail, upset child. Tom had to be there for her, comfort her and protect her. That was what he was made for, to protect his Theres from all evil, even some loud and boisterous American. He gently stroked her face and kissed away the last of her tears.

'I will have to apologize to Cecily, won't I?' Theres had composed herself. Her face was puffed, her eyes rimmed red.

'Only if you really want to. She intruded on us, so she should not be surprised to be told to get lost. If you want, I speak to her.'

'No, I was rude and I will apologize. Later.'

'You know, I think we should just try and remain by ourselves. You and me - that is what is important. Once I go back to the States, it might be a few months before we are back together. You will be busy moving to Detroit and setting up house. We will talk, but we won't be physically together. So let us just enjoy each other. What do you think?'

'But Tom, you will miss out on Bucharest if you do that. There is a guided tour and a dinner ... people will really think we are strange!'

Tom loved her for her worries.

'I can come back to Bucharest. The place will be there for another few years, I am sure. But you know, I am more interested in exploring you than I am in Bucharest.'

He leant over her and kissed her. His hand gently touched her breast below the material of her dress. Her nipple responded and he brushed against it.

'Tom! Stop it, not here!'

But then she kissed him back and they forgot their surroundings.

'I don't mind not going on the guided tour. I read about the hotel where we are staying, it sounds gorgeous, and I am sure we can have a good time there by ourselves.' Her eyes sparkled, and he knew her true self had returned.

'Now come on, dry your tears. I love you now and forever, and we are going to make the most of it!'

'Yes. Let's go for a wander in the park, the others will be another hour or so, we have plenty of time!'

The gardens had been landscaped, and they walked silently along manicured lawns amongst colorful arrays of flowers and bushes, relaxing in the warm summer sun. On their return to the coach, they saw Cecily ahead of them.

'O, Cecily', Theres called out. 'Please, wait a moment.' She rushed to the American woman and Tom followed slowly.

'Please, Cecily, let me apologize for earlier. I have not been feeling well, but that is no excuse to take it out on you. Please, forgive me?'

Cecily looked flushed, but the friendly spirit that Theres exuded caught her. She relented.

'I am sorry, too. I should have been more discreet.'

They shook hands. When Tom reached them, they smiled. He had feared the worst, but should not have worried.

'Would you like to have tea with us in our cabin before we reach Bucharest? I am sure the valet will have tidied up and made the place presentable again!'

Cecily was appeased and looking forward to spending time in the first class suite. Tom embraced Theres happily and she kissed him while Cecily looked on. Maybe the younger woman was not all that bad. Hormones, that was it, hormones and a new husband. An older husband whom she married for his money. A, the way of the world! Cecily had seen it all!

CHAPTER 19

First class was more luxurious than Cecily had expected. Decked out in dark wood and all sorts of finery, the identical cabins were nicer than her own cabin further down the carriage. It was nice to sit here, in this atmosphere of plush richness, and drink tea from real porcelain.

Theres had brought a chair from her own compartment, so they could sit at the little table. She had ordered tea and biscuits, promptly brought by their valet. The train had left Sinaia, on the short run to Bucharest.

Tom had watched Theres with concern and hoped that she was not just acting at being happy for his and Cecily's sake. Their earlier chat and the decision to skip the guided tour of the capital seemed to have made a difference to her mood. He hated to see her sad. He loved her, and would be there to dry her tears, but he preferred her to be happy. Happy with him and through him. From now on his main task in life would be to make and keep her happy.

Cecily was not as loud as they had found her earlier. She seemed impressed by their surroundings, marveling at the bathroom with its shower, and all the little extras, lacking from her cabin.

Over tea, their voices pattered along pleasantly.

'Please don't mind me asking', Cecily piped up after trying her tea. They could not have stopped her, even if her questioning had been minded.

'You two are on honeymoon, aren't you?'

Theres blushed shyly, and Tom was about to explain, when Theres agreed. She proffered her hand and waved her diamond ring about.

'That is nice', Cecily approved. She would have preferred a larger stone, but the one that Theres so happily displayed fitted her hand delicately. Theres beamed.

'Size does not always matter. Tom chose this one because it is so special. It is so extraordinary, it even has a name.'

She glanced at Tom who sat speechless and hoped for the best.

'A name? My my, that is something!' Cecily clearly was impressed.

'It is called 'Theres' heart', and that is why Tom chose it!'

Cecily admired the ring and felt a warm glow within, that only a reflection of true love could have kindled. She was happy for these two, no matter why they were together. Tears welled up, she felt alone. She wished Rupert had not died so early.

'That is so nice! I am so touched to see two people who are as happy as you two are! I wish you so much good fortune and all the happiness in the world!'

Tom sipped his tea. He did not care for this female outburst of kindness and he hoped Cecily would leave soon.

'Tell me, how long have you known each other?'

Tom coughed and spilled some tea.

'O darling, be careful!'

'Sorry, it went down the wrong hole!'

'What was your question, Cecily?' Theres had created a moment to think without making it obvious. She was clever!

'How long have you been together?'

Theres calculated, and Cecily looked at Tom who lifted a napkin to his face, and coughed again.

'Four, nearly five.... Tom, are you alright?'

'That is a long time these days. I wish you all the happiness in the world! But now I better go, I have to get ready for Bucharest. Will you join the tour and the dinner?'

Cecily busied herself with her cup and her serviette, getting up ready to leave. Tom found his voice again.

'We decided to spend the time in the hotel. As you said - honeymoon!'

Cecily shook hands and shuffled out. They locked the door behind her, and stood by the door, silently waiting till they could be sure Cecily was out of earshot. Then they burst out laughing.

'Mrs. Tom', he sounded happy.

'Mr. Theres!' She replied.

'How did you come up with the story about the diamond? And your statement about the time we have known each other was simply inspired!'

Tom pulled her to him, and they happily held each other, laughing about the conversation they had with Cecily.

'I did not lie. You would have chosen a diamond for its name and clarity, and we have been together four or five ... she assumed it to be years, I guess. But I never said!'

Her eyes sparkled again, she was happy, back with him. The wonderful woman who had stolen his heart and taken over his every thought, his every breath. Stunned into submission to her every whim, he loved it. He loved her.

CHAPTER 20

Bucharest was billed as the City of Contrasts. When they reached the station and were escorted to a taxi, Theres and Tom could not make out these contrasts.

'Another Five Star Hotel?' Tom guessed.

'This one is special, though. I have to find out a few bits, but I have plans for tonight. You will like it!'

'I sure will. So far, I have liked all the tit-bits you prepared for me. I will like this one as much as the rest.'

He cradled her in the back of the car, and became aware of the driver's watchful gaze in the mirror. The man winked, and Tom returned the gesture with a smile.

'Just got married', he said, and the man beamed.

'Congratulations! Much luck, much luck!'

Theres warmed inside. The idea of passing themselves off as a couple on honeymoon had been new, but it explained their togetherness to everyone and made their absence from group excursions more plausible. She did not mind being passed off as Mrs. Tom.

They stopped at a corner building, and a uniformed attendant opened the door of their cab.

'Welcome to the Athenee Palace Hilton Bucharest', he smiled as he exposed the glass entrance to a magnificent hall. Theres and Tom entered, speechless once more as the opulent surroundings swallowed them up. On the second floor, their room had all the necessary, deluxe amenities of a five star hotel.

'Yes, all there', Theres noted as she opened the mini-bar. 'How about a little Champagne while we make up our mind whether we want to go to the Brasserie or have sandwiches brought up by room service?'

Her earlier glum mood had evaporated completely, she was sprightly but evasive, and Tom knew she was plotting a grand surprise, something new and different from what had gone before. He loved her so much at that moment, her exuberance and sheer joyful energy. He wanted to touch her and make love to her, but she had different ideas.

'Tom, why don't you have a shower or a bath first, while I make some arrangements?'

'Won't you join me in the shower?'

'No', she said firmly. 'I have things to do!' Her emphasis was on 'to do' and there was no persuading her that her body needed refreshing as much as his. Without trying to cajole her to change her mind, he stepped into the bathroom and closed the door.

As soon as Theres heard the water and imagined Tom in the shower, she picked up the phone and called reception.

CHAPTER 21

Theres had changed into tracksuit bottoms and T-shirt when Tom came back.

'Do you have something similar?' she asked of him, and he affirmed.

'You know just as well what was on the list you sent me!'

'Good. We need to go shortly, so you better get dressed.'

She watched him take off the towel he had wrapped around his midriff. He had not dried off fully and there were little rivulets of moisture on his back, meeting at the bottom of his spine. Playfully, she approached and before he knew it, she had licked them up with the tip of her tongue. The touch made him quiver with delight and he wished she would continue, but Theres had moved on.

She never would make a good card player, her face gave her away too easily. He could not foresee what she had organized while he had showered, but he knew that the outcome of her endeavors pleased her. She was happy, and that was important. All else would fall into place, given time.

At the entrance to the hotel's own health club, they were greeted by two assistants.

'I have booked you a sauna and a massage. I can't follow you in the sauna. Firstly, it is men only, and secondly, it would not do me any good. But once you are feeling all nice and dreamy and kneaded through, just come back up to the room, I will be waiting.'

She liked giving orders, she had made plans and relied on him to stick to her schedule. He would enjoy the steam room and the massage.

'What are you going to do? You didn't dress up like that for nothing?'

'I am going for a run, they say they have some really nice treadmills here and I have missed my daily exercise since we started travelling.'

The assistants introduced themselves as Mirko and Haro, Theres introduced herself and Tom, and then Mirko led Tom away and Haro showed her to the gym. It was excellently appointed with the latest gadgetry, but Theres appreciated only the running machines. She exchanged a few words with Haro and he assured her that they would call her room as soon as Tom was ready, to give her ample warning of his return.

CHAPTER 22

With Tom out of the way, she hurriedly got the room ready. It had been the name of the hotel, Athenee Palace, that had inspired her. These days, it did not take a lot to give her ideas of this sort. Tom had opened her imagination and catapulted her along to explore and perform ever-new tricks that would please him.

When Mirko phoned to tell her that Tom was ready, she had finished the room.

The moment Tom entered, the stage in front of his eyes sucked him in. The room had been transformed. Where before the massive bed had formed the main focus, now there stood tall pillar candles in holders along the floor, illuminating a square the size of a double duvet, pillowed and cushioned. Unrecognized music played quietly in the background.

The candles flickered and threw long shadows against the walls. Behind him, he sensed Theres. She was part of the magic. She was the magic. Her voice transfixed him from the darkness.

'You have entered the Palace of Athene. Athene, the Greek goddess of wisdom, war, the arts, industry, and justice. As one of the three Olympian virgins, she is often referred to as the goddess of womankind. Tonight, this is her Palace and we are here to worship her. Take this and wear it.'

She handed Tom a large towel and watched him discard his clothes and gird it round his waist. His body still shone from the massage; she had asked Mirko to make sure that Tom would not get a chance to rub all the oil off.

'Now, go and take your place on the divan.'

Entranced, Tom moved forward. This stage set was more than he could have imagined. His feelings moved from his loin into his chest and up his throat, and he swallowed. O, Theres, wonderful Theres! Godly Theres! He had met her as a friend and now she had turned into all Womanhood. He once had read that no woman ever would be enough for a man, that there were born mothers and born lovers, born girlfriends, and born confidants, and no woman would ever fill all these different but necessary roles for any man. The writer of that article had never met someone like Theres. There only was one of her, there was none other like her in the world. His unique Theres. His Theres...

When she stepped out of the darkness, his eyes widened in wonder. She had around her a Greek-style dress, her hair layered in little tight curls and pushed up around her head, framing her brow and cascading down over her face. She carried a wide plate, careful not to spill any of its contents. Barefoot, she stepped into the ring of candles, right by his side. Then she lowered herself and he could make out the fruits and delicacies she had arranged on her platter.

'You wanted to be my slave earlier, now I am yours.' Her voice enveloped him like a dream. Tom floated, exhilarated, exuberant, gloriously happy. The vision before his eyes was magnificent. Theres, his Theres!

'Are you comfortable, my master?'

He tilted his head slightly to indicate that he was. He could not speak.

The candles shone brightly and warmed the atmosphere. Candlelight made her seem a different person, ageless again, and he eagerly believed that he was in Athene's Palace, with a silken and lush handmaiden to perform as he asked. He smiled. He would play his part!

'I could do with another for support, so I can see better.'

Theres gently leant his body forward to insert a cushion behind his back. He resumed position, and approved.

'Very well. Now for some food.'

His eyes did not leave her as she knelt between him and the platter, pointing at all the delicacies that the hotel restaurant had managed to assemble in the short time she had given them. There were sliced meats, dark bread and white, fragile butter roses, tomatoes and peppers, exotic fruits and sweets. All these she named and then awaited his further orders.

'Make me sandwiches with meat and bread and slices of tomato, and then feed me.'

Theres assembled the foodstuff as he had asked, and, he watched. She moved with a delicacy, as during their lovemaking, and it stirred him strangely. His body began to react.

He opened his mouth when she offered the bread and fillings that he had asked her to prepare. She allowed him to take a bite and again, he nodded.

'You are doing well, my little Goddess.'

Theres beamed at him, she was pleased with him as he lay there, acting out his part in her play. When he had chewed and opened his mouth a second time, she inserted the final half of the small sandwich.

'Would you like some more?' she timidly uttered, her eyes averted as became a handmaiden to the master.

'Do not rush me! I want to see you eat - take some fruit for yourself!' His voice had taken on a demanding tone. He had become her master.

Silently, she took a small sliver of fresh mango. She tilted her head back to let the juicy fruit glide into her mouth. The delicious flavor filled her and she looked again at the master. He had his eyes fixed on her, examining her every move. She looked back onto the platter and pointed wordlessly at the delicacies.

'Same again', he snarled.

Theres prepared another small mouthful for him and watched him chew and swallow.

'Is there no drink?' Tom demanded. 'Must a man choke on his bread without liquid?'

Theres stood up and got hold of a wine cooler that she had placed earlier on a table near-by. There were two glasses, but she only filled one and extended it to Tom.

'You may have some yourself', he allowed. Theres obeyed and filled the second glass and tasted the white wine. She had chosen a rich, Romanian white, highly recommended as being opulently sweet and tasty. The sommelier had been right.

Tom hummed approvingly. He pointed to the little Romanian sweetbreads that were arranged on one side of the platter.

'Let me try one of those.' Theres chose one that seemed to have a filling of nuts and marzipan and placed it in Tom's open mouth.

The room was nice and warm. When he moved, his makeshift loincloth came undone and he lay there naked. His body glistened and Theres could not avert her eyes. Under her steady gaze, his private began to stir and stand to attention like any good man of battle.

'Now look what you have done!' he growled at her teasingly. 'Move the food away, and then come and see to this fine mess!'

Theres hurriedly stood. And taking the platter away with her, walked over to the table that already accommodated the wine cooler. Excitement grabbed her and she trembled in anticipation. She knelt beside Tom's outstretched legs and waited for his orders.

'Do what you have to do! I want you to please him!' He pointed to his erection. 'After all, this is all your fault!'

Theres nodded and looked at his manhood. She loved to please him and she knew she always would. So far, their intimate unions always had been extremely fulfilling and she could see that they would continue this way.

Slowly, she cradled his testicles in their pouch and weighed them in her hands. When she looked up, Tom had closed his eyes and had sunk into the world of carnal pleasure that only she allowed him entrance to.

She spread his legs apart so she could lean into him closer, kneeling right in front of him. As delicately as she would touch a small bird, she touched him and he moaned. The sensation of her fingers moving over the soft and smooth flesh of his erect penis took his breath and made him quiver.

With her left still gently tickling his balls, her right took hold of his erection and slowly, she massaged him. Watching his face and listening to his breath and stifled little whimpers, she knew how far she had brought him, and she adapted the speed of her hand movements. Little droplets of perspiration shone on his forehead. He lay there, finding pleasure in her act, and soon she could read in his features that he was nearing his point of no return.

The pace of her hand quickened. His legs stiffened in anticipation of the release and then there it was. He shuddered and moaned and opened his eyes wide, looking at her and seeing her steady gaze on him, and he wondered what she must have thought, masturbating him without considering her own needs, making him reach the moment of ecstasy while she did all the work. He felt ashamed and fell back onto the cushions.

'Let me get a cloth', she said and when she returned, she wiped his semen off his belly and legs with a warm, moist cloth.

'I am sorry', he moaned.

'Sorry? What for?' She stood above him, looking down into his face. With some considerable effort, he brought himself to look up at her, and although he felt embarrassment, in her face there was only her love for him.

'I was greedy and egoistic.'

'You were the master and made use of your handmaiden. Get it? Hand ... maiden?' She laughed. 'Did you enjoy it?' When he nodded agreement, she replied firmly

'Good. That is all that mattered tonight.'

She untied a small bow that so far had been hidden from his view, and the dress came apart. Only then did Tom see it was a white blanket held together with some thick cord. Theres stood naked, lighted by the candlelight. Her gloriously ample curves shone and his appetite for her returned. She lay down and he cradled her in his arms.

CHAPTER 23

'This is our last day on the Orient Express', Tom said when they rejoined the train the next morning.

'I know.' Theres looked at their surroundings thoughtfully.

'Did you like the journey?' she asked.

'I loved it. I loved every single part of it. I love you.' He ran his fingers through her hair, ruffling the soft curls.

They smiled at each other, content in each other's presence. They had come a long way, in many ways.

'It will be Istanbul tomorrow. And what then?' She still had not told him, and they had another week together before he returned to the States and a life he could hardly remember. He was not looking forward to returning to his family. He wondered what his girls were doing right that moment, and glanced at his watch. Nine o'clock in the morning, they should be fast asleep back home. Safe at home.

'I thought we would stay a few days in Istanbul. I booked us a hotel in the old part of the city, close to the most famous tourist attractions. I really would like to go to the market, the bazaar, and that is not far either. And then we fly back to Scotland and I will take you to my favorite place there.'

'That sounds good. You know I will go anywhere with you, my love?' He gently squeezed her hand, as he always did when words failed him. She had noticed that before. A small gesture, but it told her so much.

They sat quietly and watched the Orient Express cross the Danube on its way south towards Bulgaria. There were no more stops now till they reached Istanbul. Their final stop.

'I read somewhere that at the bazaar, there is a whole area where you can buy cloth, and that is what I want to see', Theres explained.

'Cloth? What kind of cloth?'

'They have silks and other fine stuff. That is what the book said, and that is why Istanbul was such a target for me. A silk market of the east. I always wanted to see that.'

Tom smiled. Silk seemed of such importance to her. He could see her dressed in silk. He remembered the photograph she had sent him, of her wedding to Ben. She had worn a dark, rich red; the dress had been custom-made for her and she had looked stunning. He wished he could have seen her that day. If he had never met her before, he would have fallen in love with her then. Tom would take her to the silk market, and they would buy whatever she wanted.

'But Theres, what are you going to do with the cloth you buy?'

She tilted her head in question. 'Who says I want to buy?'

A moment's hesitation, and then she added 'I want to buy, and then make clothes from it. Did I tell you that I am a passable seamstress?'

She had not told him in so many words, but he knew that her Grandmother had been a formidable seamstress in her time. As Theres spent her first years with her grandmother, he was not surprised that she had picked up some of the essential skills of the trade.

'You never told me. Tell me now!'

He longed to hear her speak of her past, of her early experiences, to sit and listen and take it all in. He so needed to be part of her, even if it was just by her talking.

'I got my first sewing machine when I was five. For Christmas. It was an old one, and it only ever managed straight lines. Grandma gave it to me, as I always had been interested in her machine, ever since I was really little. But the one I got was so heavy that I could hardly lift it myself. It was an old Singer, and it came in this heavy, hard carry case. I became really good at it, sewing clothes for all my dolls. Once I even machine-stitched a butterfly on a scarf I made for this special dolly. I will show you pictures some day, I have kept them. The machine still exists. But you know, not only was I good at sewing with it, I also was real good at taking it apart. I would unscrew the outer casing, and then explore the inner workings. By the time I was six or seven, I could do the full maintenance of the machine, just by looking and investigating.'

Tom could see her, a small girl with blond hair, lifting the heavy machine and then taking tools to it to take it apart. Her imagery was lively and so vivid that he could see the clothes she had designed for her dolls. His Theres. He took pride in her achievements, even though he had not been involved in them. Then he remembered that when she was seven, he already was thirty and married. The thought appalled him. He shivered.

'You okay?' Theres had noticed the little cloud of apprehension throw a shadow over his smile, and she had picked up on it immediately.

'I am fine. Tell me more!' He did not want to explain to her his uneasiness about her young years, the difference in their age, as he knew she would brush any concerns aside. The thought would soon leave and not take hold of him for long.

'There is nothing more to tell. I got several other machines since, but I never had this intimate knowledge and quiet confidence like I had with the first one. Must have been my first love, they say that stays with you forever.'

Once the thought settled, he could not help himself but ask: 'And who was your first love, Theres? Would you tell me that?'

Theres looked at him, wondering what she should say. She knew that Tom needed to understand her better, and she happily told him what he wanted to know.

'There was a boy at school, when I was about 14. I think he liked me, too, for he came to see me at weekends. But we never made a big deal of it all, so hardly anybody knew about it. It was really strange. When we moved away, he sent me a letter saying that he felt we could no longer see each other. Which, I suppose, was right enough. When I was seventeen, he found me again and we started seeing each other for the second time. But I broke it off. When I was nineteen, I got in touch with him, and we spent a beautiful summer together. Only to drift apart at the end of it.'

'Did you love him?'

'I thought so, at the time, but there were always things that we never spoke about. We never seemed to spend time with others, it was always just 'us', and he seemed to be reluctant to tell his friends about me. Maybe he was worried that they might give him grief about me, I don't know.'

'Maybe he just wanted you to himself?'

'Like you, you mean?' She knew how he felt. He wanted to be with her and not share her, for she meant so much to him and time was so precious.

'Like I!'

They laughed and joined hands and sat in silence again.

'Is Lillian your first love?'

'What makes you think of Lillian?'

'You think of Lillian, that is what.' O, how she knew him! She could read him so easily! Yes, it was true, he had thought of Lillian and his girls again, and he was worried about their well being. But he wanted to concentrate on Theres, his Theres, his Queen, his Magic, his Woman, his All.

'I always thought she was. But we have been married so long that it sometimes is very hard to define the feelings that are there. I don't want to talk about it, I want to talk about us!'

'But Tom, there is no 'us' as long as you are thinking about Lillian. And don't you think I have a right to know what you are feeling towards her?'

She was right, but he felt uncomfortable. His words might hurt his Theres and so he chose them carefully.

'We are getting on all right. We have made a good life together, it is well defined, and there is Jenny and Megan. But what there is lacking is the excitement, the little shudders that run across me when you touch me, or when I hear your voice or your laughter. Our life has always been in a straight line, never any surprises, and I am learning now that what I sometimes thought missing, as lacking and even unreal, the depths of emotions we share – it all can exist. It exists now, for you and me!'

'Do you still sleep with her?'

'Theres ...'

'Do you?'

'I did before. It will be different now.'

'How will it be different?'

'You have made the difference. I had never been with a woman that makes love to me like you do. You have been an experience for me, you still are. You made me new again, and you taught me a lot. I always thought that the things we experience when we are intimate together were confined to the realms of erotic fiction. Not open to me. Now I know different, and I am not sure how this is going to affect my life with Lillian.'

Theres sat and listened. Making love to Tom had been more than good, he had been so keen and willing to follow her wherever she had led him, and she had adored him for it. At the same time, she knew of the changes and there was no going back to a time 'before', not even for her and Ben.

'And you still sleep with Ben?'

'Of course, he is my husband.'

'Why is Jenny staying with you and Lillian?'

'Why do you ask that?'

'I ask because I could not live with my parents, or even my grandparents, no matter how much I love them. It would be really claustrophobic. Doesn't she have a life of her own? Does she see men?'

'She has Megan, and we all share in looking after her. That is enough for Jenny, and it is nice for us as well. What are you saying?'

'I am saying that Jenny is in her early thirties, and she has needs beyond those you, Lillian and even Megan can fulfil for her. If nothing else, she must miss sex.'

'Theres, you are crude! Jenny is ... happy!'

'Is she seeing someone? No? I wouldn't be surprised if she did, only you don't know because she is too worried of what it would do to you if you knew. Or her if you did not approve. And approve you would not, as no man would be good enough for her.'

'Theres - how can you say these things?'

'They just come out, to be honest. They are things I have been wondering about for a while. All I am saying - I could not live with mum and dad or my father, I rather starve!'

For the first time that they were together, an uneasy silence fell over them. Tom knew Jenny was happy and he knew that she had a good life under his protection in his house. One day, she would meet a nice man, and she would leave, but for the time being, she was safely at home and they were happy together!

'Lunch?'

'Is it that time already?'

'Yes. And Tom?'

'Yes?'

'What I said...'

'Forget it!'

'How can I? It is in my mind and I spoke freely. I wish you could see that I mean nothing bad.'

Tom took her in his arms. He needed her touch and at this very moment, she needed his. They needed each other.

'I know, my love. You would not mean anything bad. But Jenny is happy. One day, you will meet her and find out for yourself!'

CHAPTER 24

Lunch had been rainbow trout, rice and fresh petit pois, followed by ice cream. Conversation had ebbed without ever regaining full flow. Far away with their thoughts, Tom and Theres could not share just yet. The end loomed. They were sad.

The pianist had entertained them whenever they joined the dining car or the bar. He now sat at his upright, playing away at a selection of classical and modern pieces. Theres thought him to be Hungarian, his features reminded her of Ferenc from Budapest and she remembered little Gretha. Would the little girl remember her? She so wished she had taken their address, but neither had they offered nor did she ask. Gretha was lost to her forever, only a bright memory left. Not for the first time or the last, she wondered if she would ever be blessed with a little Gretha of her own.

Tom watched the Bulgarian countryside for a while. His thoughts were back home, and he wondered how he would explain the absence of souvenirs and photographs. He was not good at lying and needed to think up a plausible excuse to explain his whereabouts.

'Tom?'

'Yes, my dear?'

'Tom, this is still part of our journey, isn't it?'

'Yes, it most certainly is.'

'Do you remember what we said, that we would enjoy every step and every moment we had together?'

'Yes, I do remember that!'

'Then let us not be gloomy. I am sorry I said what I did, but we always have spoken openly and honestly. I don't want my cynicism hang over the remainder of the journey. Can we forget it?'

'Forget what, my love?'

'Thank you. I love you, you know?'

'I know. And I love you, too!'

Their hands touched across the table, and the warmth of before returned. The feeling started deep inside, between their breasts and their navels, at the solar plexus, the center of all being, the seat of the very soul. It rose, engulfed and swept them away to a time and a place that held only them. They lost the feeling for their surroundings, and beheld only each other. This was the present, this was their now. This was their love for each other.

A waiter brought coffee. Still there were no words, just the deep and enveloping sense of togetherness. The pianist played a joyful tune, and Theres awakened.

'Remember when you said that you would slow-waltz me across Texas?'

'Yes, I do remember that.'

'How about starting right now?'

Tom looked around. Most of the other couples had retreated, there were few people around. The pianist seemed to be playing for them alone, and he would appreciate their attention to his art.

'Yes, I would like that', and he watched as Theres strode over to the piano and exchanged some words with the musician. He smiled at her, nodded at Tom and began to play slow, melodic tunes that befitted their mood.

Theres stood and waited for Tom in the little square beside the piano, where they had seen other passengers dance. The space was not wide, but it was more than they required. He put his right arm tightly around her waist, and her right hand in his left. He pulled her close, and they began to move with the music. They were close, no blade could have separated them. Her head rested against his cheek, she had closed her eyes and relied on him to keep her safe.

Their audience of two other couples watched; and, then, one after the other, they left, touched by the display of newly wedded bliss. Theres, Tom and the pianist were the only occupants of the bar car. Theres and Tom were alone in a world that only had room for them. The music was an added bonus, but they had their own inner music.

So they moved with the rhythm, but hardly moved at all. Their embrace tightened, their feelings soared. One song came to an end and a new one took its place, but they did not notice. Waiters came and cleared the remainders of lunch from the tables and set up for dinner. After three more songs, the pianist stopped and watched as Theres and Tom kept moving on the little dance floor. The musician left and they did not notice. They slow-waltzed across Texas, forever in each other's arms, as the Orient Express continued across Bulgaria toward Istanbul.

CHAPTER 25

Eventually, they became aware of their music-less dancing. Tom cupped her face and kissed her gently and fully on the lips.

'I love you, my Theres. I want to be with you forever!'

Theres clasped his hands with hers and wrapped herself back into his arms.

'I would like that.'

They stood in a tender embrace.

'Shall we go back to our cabin?' he asked throatily.

Theres took him and he followed her to where they could be by themselves, locked away from prying eyes of other occupants of the train.

'Tom, how did you mean that when you said you wanted to be with me forever?'

She dared not look at him, too much depended on his answer. Since their journey started, she had known that she wanted to be with nobody but Tom, but had felt too afraid to ask him his true emotions in case she would spoil what they had.

They made comfortable on the settee in his cabin, his arms around her shoulder, Theres leaning into him so that he could smell her hair, but not see her face. Talking about difficult things was easier without eye contact.

'I meant what I said - I want to be with you forever.'

'What about Lillian and the girls?'

He sighed, and thus unveiled his anguish to her.

'I will have to go back. So will you have to go back to Ben. But there will always be a part of me that will be with you, and you with me.'

'So you don't mean we will be physically together, it's all metaphorical and we will just dream about it?'

'We will have to wait and see, I think. You will need to pack up and move to Detroit. Once you are there, I will come and visit and stay with you as often as possible. I will find a way. But I might have to go back.'

'Will you really have to?'

'I don't know. I know I want to be with you, but it might be difficult to leave the girls behind. No matter what you think, they need me, they are not as strong and spirited as you are. I have always looked after them, I have been brought up that way, and I will never stop feeling responsible for them. But I will always love you, I know that now, and I will do the best I can to be with you as often as possible.'

'I might not like that, I don't know whether I can share you like that.'

'I have to share you with Ben, isn't that the same?'

'Ben was not even sure whether he would come to Detroit with me, and I will tell him that I don't want him to come. I could not lie to him and pretend I still have feelings for him if all I care for is you!'

The train was moving fast, so Tom could only see smears of colors as he glanced outside.

'You know I love you, but I am worried that one day you will leave me, and find someone who can give you more than I do. I want to take this risk, and believe me, to me this risk is great. For however long we have together, I want to make the most of it.'

'O, Tom … I am so happy when I am with you. Nobody ever touched me like you do, you fill my heart and my soul! In the mornings, when I wake up, the first thing that comes to my mind is you. In the evenings, I fall asleep thinking about you … I hear what you say about me and finding someone else, but I wouldn't even look for someone else, you are all I would want if only you could be mine!'

He pulled her close, as words failed him.

'I love you, my precious Theres!'

'And I will remain patient and hope that one day, you will be all mine and I won't have to share you!'

They sat in silence once more, hearts quietly weeping over an uncharted future. For now, they marveled at their attachment and felt their souls rejoice in fragile union.

Evening came and they heard the faint sound of the bell, calling the passengers to dinner.

'I am not hungry', Theres stated and Tom had to agree. Later, they would ask for cheese and biscuits to be brought to their compartment, much later.

Theres shifted, and Tom let her body fall to rest on his lap. His hands caressed the crown of her head, and twirled her gentle curls. His thighs bore her weight pleasurably, and he did not want her to move.

Darkness moved in on them slowly.

'It is our last night here tonight', she said.

'I know.'

'You know what I would like to do?'

'Tell me, please do.'

He could spend hours just touching her this way, the softness of her hair and the gentleness of her skin. For a brief moment, he wondered if he could satisfy her a whole night long, but she surprised him once again when she explained her wishes to him.

'I would like to sit up and read. I take a chapter, and then you take another. This way, we can fill the night and we won't have to go asleep till we both are too tired to continue. And then we can just lie on this settee, hold each other, and rest, with our clothes on, till we have to get up in Istanbul and leave.'

'Is that what would please you?'

'Yep.'

'And what book would you like to read?'

'How about Great Expectations? Dickens?'

'Are you sure this is what you want for our last night on this train?'

Theres nodded.

'Then this is what we shall do.'

They moved to the table and Theres went to get a well-read and well-loved copy of the book. She read to him in her clear and distinct voice about Master Pip and the man he met at the cemetery. The story evolved, brought to life by her voice. They were introduced to the strange but lovely Estella and the haughty Miss Havisham. When her voice tired, Tom read for a while till Theres took the book off him. So it went. In the early hours of the morning, her head came to rest on her arms, and Tom knew she had fallen asleep.

He pushed his chair back quietly, lifted her to her feet, and guided her to the settee. She followed meekly, not quite certain what was going on. Once he had settled her on his bed, he lay down beside her and cradled her in his arms, fully dressed, as she had asked. His desire rose with her touch, but he let her sleep, there in his arms. So they spent their last night together on the Orient Express, approaching Istanbul, Theres in dreamless slumber, and Tom in watchful waking, until he joined her in sleep.

CHAPTER 26

'Theres! Wake up!' She was fast asleep, still in his arms. He loved to wake up next to her, the last thing at night, and first thing in the morning, to be with her. His Theres, always his Theres!

Slowly, she stirred. When she saw him leaning over her, she smiled. Her first smile of the day. It was for him, and he loved her for it. But it was ten o'clock, and they had to get ready for leaving, later, in the afternoon. They had to get showered, get changed and packed.

Theres stretched and pulled his face close. She kissed him. She did not seem to mind that he had not cleaned his teeth. So he gave in and kissed her back, passionately.

'My love, we have slept in. It is time to get up and get ready!'

Theres nodded, still sleepy, and pushed past him. Standing, she stretched again; and, in a flash, turned into the feline he had seen in her before.

'That is better! Do you want the bathroom first?' she asked. She was beautiful first thing in the morning. To him, she was beautiful any time!

'Yes, if you don't mind. I won't be long!'

'Take your time. I will pop into mine, just give me a nod when you are ready!'

She walked away and he got on with his morning toilet.

They skipped breakfast and took lunch instead. As everybody got ready to leave, the meal was slightly less lavish than had been standard previously. They had to make do with grilled chicken and vegetables. They did not stay for coffee or dessert, but returned to their cabin.

Theres insisted on packing, separating his effects from hers. When he went to check on her progress in her cabin, she had flung clothes everywhere, and was considering which dresses she would keep towards the top of her case for wearing in Istanbul.

'Why do you need to wear anything? We could just stay in the hotel room, and indulge in each other?' Theres looked at him and that look shut him up.

'Maybe not', he felt himself forced to say, and retreated. He had been sitting on the settee for a while, continuing to read the story of the previous night, when Theres eventually sauntered over.

'Done', she exclaimed, as she threw herself onto the settee.

'What are you doing?'

'Reading your book!'

'Do you like it? It's my favorite classic. I have read it so often, I can't remember how many times!'

'I can see the dog ears!' he laughed.

'My mother always said that it was disrespectful to mark pages by bending them over. But I think it shows your love and your ease with the book when you do that, so I have taken to mark the books I like with dog ears!'

Tom looked at her. Slowly and purposefully, he bent the page he had been reading when she had entered his cabin.

'What time do you think we will be getting into Istanbul?'

'About four, maybe before then.'

'We have plenty of time to make love on this settee one more time...'

Theres thought. There was a subtle knock and Tom looked at her in surprise.

'Expecting anybody?'

'No, I don't think so!'

Tom got up and opened the door to Cecily.

'Hi, sorry to intrude like this...'

'Cecily, come in! We were just wondering what to do next. Have you finished packing?'

Cecily entered and nodded.

'Yes. I do travel light. I just came to say my 'Good byes' and to let you know that whenever you are in Cleveland, Ohio, to just pop your head in. You would always be welcome!'

Theres took the older woman's hands. Cecily, attired in a gaudy, bright caftan, had prepared for the experience of Istanbul. Theres had no doubt Cecily would completely submerge herself in the mystique of the Orient, and come away with stories about international espionage and swanky suitors.

'That is very kind of you', Tom responded.

'And how do we find you in Cleveland, Ohio?' asked Theres.

Cecily hesitated.

'Just look me up in the phonebook. Cecily de Houten, there is only one number with this name, there are no other de Houten's in Cleveland, Ohio. Come and see me whenever you can! And now I must go. Have a pleasant stay in Istanbul!'

Like a gust of wind, Cecily swept away. Theres laughed at Tom.

'You know, my love, when Americans invite you to their homes like that, they don't necessarily mean it', he instructed her.

'I know, that is why I asked how we would find her.'

'You are so direct and open, I sometimes fear for you, my love.'

'Do not fear, I will be all right. But tell me once more - do you mean what you say to me when you speak of your love and our future?'

'How can you ask me that? Of course I do! O come here, let me embrace you, let me hold you close and kiss you and then you will never ever be able to doubt me again!'

He wrapped her into his embrace, and there she remained. The last chance of making love on the Orient Express had vanished, there would always be tomorrow and the next day and the next day after that.

CHAPTER 27

When the train pulled into Istanbul, chaos swallowed them as soon as they stepped onto the station platform. The valet had warned them not to leave their luggage unattended, so Theres sent Tom to look out for the Ambassador Hotel representative, while she remained to watch after their assorted cases and bags.

Someone called out his name, and Tom soon found himself with his guide and two porters from the hotel. The man welcomed him, inquired in pleasantly intoned English about his journey and his new wife. Tom introduced him to Theres, who had waited in their cabin, and they left together. Cecily waved at them from a distance. Before they walked away from the Orient Express, Tom walked back to the line of waiters and valets and shook their hands, handing over dollar bills to each. Theres had not discussed this, but it pleased her to see his show of savoir faire. These people had offered good service, had played along nicely with their notions, had helped with midnight picnics, and waited on them in their cabin whenever they asked. They deserved a generous tip.

'Why did you choose the hotel we are at?' Tom asked in the taxi. 'It is called the Ambassador, so not really an inspiring name, not like the last one?'

Theres giggled, remembering Athene's Palace. 'No, I chose it solely because it is close to all the sights. It is right in the center of downtown 'Sultan Ahmet', the historic part of town. Apparently, the views are breathtaking. We will see!'

The Ambassador did not disappoint. The hotel was less luxurious than their previous lodgings, but the public rooms were appointed with all modern amenities. Their pleasant suite would make a good base for their excursions over the next few days.

After unpacking the bare necessities, they relaxed quietly for a few moments. Later, they went to the rooftop terrace restaurant where they spent the evening, drinking in the atmosphere, opening the doors of their senses to the door to the East.

CHAPTER 28

The night was stuffy and sleep had come slowly. The air-conditioner toiled, and the fan hummed monotonously over-head, trying its utmost to stir the air in their room. Their naked bodies glistened with sweat and their love.

Theres woke suddenly with a jolt. Tom tossed about and she turned to hug him.

'Sh, my love, just a bad dream.'

He woke and looked at her. 'Theres, I am sorry.'

'A bad dream?' He nodded, vaguely. 'Want to tell me about it?'

Tom rolled away from her and onto his back. He stretched his arm out for her, and she assumed the position she loved, her ear close to his heart, where she could hear it beat strongly, in rhythm with her own. For a while, Tom stroked her back silently, running his fingers slowly up and down, the way he knew she liked.

'It is nothing, really.'

'Tom, why don't you phone home tomorrow, just to see that they are all okay.'

Theres had noticed Tom's growing unease. He thought about home without actually telling her, but she understood. She knew it was up to her to acknowledge his dilemma. It hurt, she felt extremely jealous of the other women in his life, and yet she had to either live with their existence or let him go. That, she could not do. She loved Tom too much. But he suffered and mulled over their future and the tenability of his life between Lillian and Theres. There was no easy way out. The horns of his dilemma dug into him and the pain caused nightmares.

'I didn't want to say, and now I realize I should have told you what I feel. I think it would make things easier for me if I just could say 'hi' and tell them that I was okay.'

'So tomorrow, around lunch, we find a phone somewhere and you call them. And then we enjoy the next few days.'

'Won't you mind?'

'Tom, don't be silly, I rather have you call your wife than worry and make me all fidgety. Come here, let's get back to sleep.'

CHAPTER 29

On the magnificent rooftop terrace, over-looking the dome of Ayasofia, the Blue Mosque with its six graceful minarets, and the waters of Marmara, waiters served breakfast. Early in the day, the haze of summer still lay over the city, and the busy streets remained a distant hum, increasing with the hours of the day. The muezzin, who had called the believers to the first prayers of the morning, ended their night early. Tom and Theres stepped onto the terrace, and greeted another glorious day. They felt surprisingly refreshed and had the whole of the day to look forward to.

While the believers met and bowed their heads towards Mecca, Tom and Theres had made love, silently and passionately. He had needed to feel her, had needed to watch her face as he entered her and had not wanted to let her go after his lust was exhausted. Their union had been swift but satisfying, at least for him. Theres did not seem to mind. It would be her turn that evening, he wanted it to be that way, did not want her to be left out and remain unfulfilled. He would be looking forward all day to the moment when he would watch her reach her ecstasy. When he would be there to watch her whole body shudder, the little screams that were of joy, but could just as easily be of pain. Thoughts of Theres' climax nearly made him hard a second time. He wished he had met her a long time ago. Then he remembered. Twenty years earlier, he would have asked for sex with a thirteen- year-old.

After the culinary excesses of the last week, Theres and Tom partook of fruit, juice and coffee only. All was fresh and inviting. The hotel had organized a tour guide for them, and a young man, Suleyman, made himself known to them as they finished their breakfast. In his early twenties with shiny black hair and olive-colored skin, he spoke passable English. Tom sat back and watched Theres as she haggled with Suleyman over his expenses for the day. She had chosen their activities carefully, so the first half of the day should be spent wandering the market quarter. Theres expressed a particular interest in fine cloth and silk. Tom was only too willing to please her, as he would please her in other ways later on.

The bazaar was no more than a short walk away. The pavements were busy, the day had begun in earnest while they sat and spoke with Suleyman about their travels and the route that had brought them to Istanbul. To the young Turk, they were rich, and he hoped for considerable baksheesh. Theres told him in no uncertain terms that he would have to do very well to justify their gratitude; she only expected the best of their hired hands. Tom had been impressed. She could behave like a Lady, a true Lady, when the moment required it, and she easily managed to slip into other roles as and when the mood took her.

Street merchants crowded in on them as soon as they reached the bazaar. Suleyman negotiated their way, making certain they were not harassed too frighteningly. Theres' blond hair and voluptuous body made her an easy and exciting target. Her smile asked forgiveness for not buying from anybody holding their ware in her face. But she had no money on her this day; Tom was the keeper of their finances. He wore a money pouch tightly under his shirt, and only had a few coins in his pockets. With Suleyman's help and protection, they would be safe.

The bazaar lived up to their expectations. Tourists and natives joined in the atmosphere, reeking of a heady mix of spices, exotic foods, and the sweat of many people. Past the bookseller's market, they entered the Grand Bazaar, where sixty narrow streets joined, fronted by thousands of shops. Suleyman looked out for Theres and Tom, making sure not to lose them in the crowd. For Theres, the smells and sounds both excited and overpowered. She felt dizzy and held on tight to Tom, who kept his arm protectively around her shoulder. If he lost her in the throng, he was sure she would end up in some rich Arab's harem, never to be seen or heard of again.

They fought their way past the goldsmiths, the pearl merchants, the carpet and antique dealers. People stared at Theres. Tom worried possessively as he safeguarded her.

The walk was exciting and the impressions manifold. When eventually they reached the area where traders of fine cloth were located, Theres looked around in wonderment. She had always dreamt of visiting the cloth markets of the East, but had never imagined seeing this many beautiful materials, these fine cottons and linens. But the stalls that caught her attention merchandised silks.

It was one particular stall to which Suleyman led them. Maybe the owner was his uncle, or Suleyman was on a commission, but that did not matter to Theres. The merchant had arrayed an exquisite quality and magnificent variety of shades. Here, she ran her hands along the bales, feeling and letting her fingers decide which one to look at more closely. Everyone could see her joy at that moment. That she could be this ecstatic when not alone with him caused a pang of envy in Tom's heart. At the same time, her happiness elevated and elated him. This was what life should be all about.

The merchant followed Theres closely, while Tom and Suleyman stood back and marveled at her discrimination. She picked out bale after bale. The merchant stacked an extraordinary pile on a counter. She walked through the aisles again and again. When she finally had enough, she called Tom and Suleyman over.

'O, Tom, this is heaven! Now help me chose, please?' The child within possessed her. Theres could move from being totally in control to being as joyful as any five-year old. He could only stand in wonder, as he realized this woman's endless capacity to amaze him.

Theres had chosen a mixture of wild and shiny-smooth silks of different hues. One after the other, she unrolled enough material to hold it around her, so he could see how it would complement her. Suleyman motioned the shopkeeper to stay away and let them play a little without being forced into buying. He had promised the man that there would be a sale, but the moment had not yet come.

'How about this one?' Theres draped a rich, dark plum-colored fabric over her shoulder. When she turned, it reflected in the sunlight, and he could see her wearing a full-length robe. She would be a Lady again, her hair would be curled up tightly around her head, and she would be the belle of his ball.

'I love that. Whatever you do, buy some of this. I can see you already wearing a dress made from this color.' She was beautiful. She would look beautiful in sackcloth.

'What about that green one? That would look nice on you, too. Or that red one?'

'Now that I think of it, I have a silk frock made from a similar shade, so maybe not the red one. I really like the orange, but orange is not really my color.' When she held it against her breast, she added: 'Makes me look ill, don't you think?'

They had forgotten the world around them, busy deciding, when the merchant came and brought forth a bale dyed with a very special effect. Subtle color changes, from purple to pink and orange, enlivened the material beyond sheer brilliance.

'Yes', she gasped. 'That is IT! How could I not have seen this straight away?' She unrolled length after length and draped herself into it. Suleyman, the merchant, and Tom applauded, concurring. The hues accentuated and enhanced her own beauty. Tom saw the dress she would wear. His Theres.

'Suleyman, come here', she ordered. 'Can you translate for me? I want to buy now!'

The young man nodded. He had been looking forward to this part of the morning.

'This purple material? I want five meters of it. How much?'

Suleyman consulted with the merchant.

'Fifty Dollars.'

'US?' The merchant nodded. 'Forget it. For that, I can buy back home. For that, I don't need to come to Istanbul. Too much and the man knows it!'

Suleyman spoke again. 'There has been a misunderstanding. He thought you wanted 10 meters. The price is twenty-five dollars.'

'Tell him, I will give him fifteen, and that is too much. But I feel happy today, so I will be generous.'

More hushed words in Turkish, a sly smile from the merchant, and then a nod. He held out his right hand three times. 'Ten and five. Dollars. US.'

Theres liked bargaining. She knew she could have had the silk for ten Dollars, but she felt good, so she did not mind. She turned to Tom, who had watched intently all the while, and she smiled. He returned her smile, and retreated deeper into the shop, away from the glances of passers-by, to retrieve some of the money carried beneath his shirt.

'Now, Suleyman, tell the man that I want ten meters from this material', and she put her hand on the bale of many colors.

The merchant started a tirade of noisy words, singing his praise of her choice and good taste. Theres did not need an interpreter to give her the meaning of his speech.

'Suleyman, tell him that he should give me this material for free as it so obviously needs to be made into a dress for a woman like myself, to show it off and to give it some of my beauty and status. But tell him also, that I am feeling gracious today and therefore, I will pay him twenty Dollars.'

The man evidently understood as he shook his hand. 'No, no twenty Dollars. Forty Dollars. Good silk.'

Theres in turn waved her hands at him in disapproval. 'Forty is too much. Not good enough for forty. Twenty-five. And I will tell all my friends to come here and buy off him and what a good, honest man he is.'

Suleyman stepped in and whispered into the man's ear. Whatever he said, it changed the merchant's mind, and he accepted twenty-five dollars. He cut the material under Theres' watchful eyes, careful not to short-measure her. When he gave her the carefully secured parcel, Tom came forward, paid him in cash and they left. She knew the merchant got more money than he would have from a local buyer. He was happy.

As their shopping had taken a lot longer than anticipated, Tom asked the guide to take them back to the hotel. They would rest for an hour, before continuing their sight seeing later in the afternoon.

Theres clutched her paper bag of silks. She liked the atmosphere of Istanbul, the way people looked at her, and the way Tom held her protectively close. For that, she loved him. She would sew a beautiful dress, and she would wear it to the ball and Tom would be her beau. One day. She was happy.

▪▪

Chapter 30

On their return to their suite, they found the bed had been made and a fresh basket of fruit and flowers left on the sideboard. Theres kicked off her shoes and threw herself onto the bed.

'You know', Tom said,' for once, I have an idea of what we do next. You just wait there, don't go away!'

He locked himself into the bathroom, and Theres could hear water running in the bathtub. She smiled. Tom had come a long way in his thinking. The superbly furnished corner bath would hold two people, and she had wondered whether she could entice him once more to a new experience. Budapest, when they showered together, arose in her mind. This time, he seemed to have thought of something exciting all by himself.

The bathroom door opened a crack, and his arm appeared. His fingers beckoned her to enter.

The door shut behind her, and the room was in darkness. She could hear Tom breathe, could smell perfume and hot water, and feel his body next to hers.

'Trust me', he whispered.

****

His hands felt for her arms and pulled her closer to him. Running his hands slowly across her body, he gently unbuttoned the top of her dress and let it fall to the floor. He unhooked the eyelets of her bra. Then he bent down and pulled her panties off. Her eyes became accustomed to the darkness, and she could make out the diamond reflections of foam in the bathtub, and smelled the rich aroma of perfume. She could make out Tom next to her and realized that he, too, was naked. She wanted to hold him, but he took her hand and guided her forward to the bath.

'Careful now. And try first, but I don't think it is too hot for you.'

The water's temperature was just perfect, and she glided into its warm, watery embrace. When Tom stepped in after her, water slopped over the edge. Theres giggled. Sitting in the warm water, with Tom's nakedness so close, the lights turned off and only the faintest illumination, she shivered. He knew the effect of his preparation on her. She knew he had come to love surprising her. This was excellent.

'Here, let me wash you.' Tom leant forward, so that his face was close to hers. In his hand, he held her sponge and he now started to gently rub it over her shoulders and arms.

'This is nice', she whispered.

'For now, I am going to be your slave. I am going to wash you and then I will dry you and take you to bed. Where I will make love to you whichever way I want.'

Theres inhaled with a hiss. His touch was sensual and she felt a growing need for his body close to hers, for the physicality of their union and she knew she would have to have him before long. Tom did not lack for imagination. At this moment, she became his Queen Sheba, and he became her slave. Theres shivered with desire.

'Tom?'

'Shh, my love, be silent.'

'I want you. Now.'

'Shh. This is not an option. Yet. You are dirty after the day out walking in the bazaar, and I need to cleanse your body first before I can love you.'

He massaged her tummy with the sponge, leaving out her breasts. He would make sure that they, too, would be clean. In a little while.

He sat back and took hold of her right foot. She wriggled as she was ticklish; and, again, he hushed her. Gently, he sucked her big toe into his mouth. Carefully, he flicked his tongue over and all around it. He heard her gasp and knew that she longed for his touch elsewhere. His mouth moved from toe to toe till he kissed her pinky. He expended the same treatment on her left. Theres lay back, her arms on the rims of the bath. She submersed herself in his touch. She did not want to wake up from this moment.

Having thoroughly cleaned her feet with his tongue, Tom continued to minister to her legs. With circular motions, he rubbed the sponge along her shins, her calves, up higher and higher till he reached the sensitive flesh of her inner thighs. She quivered in anticipation, and he took great care not to waken her shiny pearl with his touch.

'And now your back', he hissed and she leant into him, her face touching his shoulder. He reached around her, and sponged her shoulders, and down her spine as far as he could reach.

'What about you, don't you need to be cleansed?' Theres suggested.

'No, I am all right. This is for you alone.'

He continued; her breasts buoyed on the scented cushion of water. Her nipples pushed against the sponge, hard and erect. He longed to touch them with his lips, but restrained himself. He took his time running the sponge leisurely around each swollen bud, relishing the sensations deep within his own body. He loved her nakedness, in darkness as in light. The lightlessness in the bathroom allowed him to visualize her before his inner eye, and he could see her in all her womanly glory. His princess, his Theres.

The sponge had one rough side, and he gently made use of that, performing his duties on her inner secret. She whimpered, and opened her legs for him as wide as she could, lifting one leg onto the side of the bath. Water dripped off her toes onto the tiles. Up and down, he rubbed with a sensitive hand. The fabric of the sponge added to the erotic titillation as he performed these arpeggios. The tunnel of her love was overflowing, and she felt the build-up of a glorious climax. When he ceased, she protested meekly.

'Not here, later.' He decided to be hard with her; for once he wanted to have things his own way.

He stood up and made her turn below him. Touching her rear had been something he had envisaged, but never dared to ask for. He sponged the puckered rose that he more imagined than saw. Running the sponge over her cheeks, he gently stroked with his other hand. Theres did not reject his touch. His prick jerked up and the need to enter Theres became stronger with each moment's delay. He had to be strong not to force himself on her. Their lovemaking had been reckless at times, but he respected her too much to dwell on this thought. For a while he was absorbed in stroking her, but he could not bring himself to enter her from behind. There might come a time, but only if she gave explicit permission.

Before she knew it, Tom had left the bath. When she stood, he wrapped her into a large towel, helping her step out.

'Careful, it is wet here and I don't want you to slip on the tiles.'

CHAPTER 31

Golden sunshine swathed their room. They emerged from their bath, infused with longing and mutual desire. Tom led the way towards the massive bed, when Theres stopped.

'What is that?' She pointed at a white slip of paper on the floor next to the entrance door. Tom shook his head, walked over and picked it up.

'A letter from reception, I think.'

Theres held out her hand. 'Give it to me, I have a look. And why don't you phone home, and just check on your girls?'

'You mean...'

'I mean we will rest easier and can relax more once you know that all is well. Let me deal with whatever that letter wants, and you make your call.'

It relieved Tom that Theres should have remembered. He didn't want any interference while making love to her, but the mood had already been broken with the note pushed under their door, so he might as well.

The phone rang at the first go. It was 1:00 PM in Istanbul and 7:00 AM at his house in the States. Jenny would still be asleep, but Megan and Lillian should be up. On the second ring, his call was answered. It was Jenny and he felt an immediate alarm.

'Dad! I am so glad you are phoning!' There were tears in her voice and horror overcame Tom, a sensation of something dreadful having happened while he was happy here with Theres.

'Jenny? Jenny, tell me, what is going on?'

Theres looked up. She could sense the tremor in his voice, and the hairs on the back of her neck stood on end.

'Dad, it is Megan. She is in hospital and she needs an emergency operation. I only just got back from there, Mom is still with her and I am going back after I had a shower and grabbed some of her things...'

'Jenny - what is wrong?'

'O Dad...' her voice trailed away in tired, desperate sobs.

Theres was there, behind him, holding on to him or he might have fallen. He put the phone down and slowly turned towards her, tears in his eyes. Theres knew that he had made his choice.

'I need to go', he whispered. 'They need me at home.'

Silently, she nodded. She always had known that it would end like this. There was no real future for them. It all had been stolen time. Her stomach contracted, she felt physically sick, but Theres did not show him her desperate hurt. She had lost the game, maybe even had lost him forever.

'You better pack', she said. 'I will organize a taxi to the airport.'

Suleyman had sent the note, letting them know he would wait on the roof terrace. Theres went to find him, and explained that her husband had to return to the States straight away. She needed his help to secure an immediate flight. The young Turk read the situation, saw her distress, and knew better than to offer his support for anything else. He took orders and found a phone. When Tom had finished packing his case, a taxi already waited.

Silently, Theres and Tom clambered in the back; Suleyman sat next to the driver, chatting. Tom held her hand, his mind far away, wondering whether he would be in time. He suddenly hated the distance between himself and his little girl. He should have been there ... she needed him now, and he was here, with Theres. In that instance, their liaison lost its sparkle. Through the veil of his tears, he looked at Theres. She still was beautiful, he still loved her, but there was something else now. He should not be here, with her; he should be at home!

The ride to the airport took only half an hour, as the driver seemed not to care for red lights or speed restrictions. Suleyman had instructed him to be as quick as possible. There was baksheesh in it for him if he was quick.

The taxi stopped, and Suleyman paid the driver before guiding Theres and Tom to the Turkish Airlines booking desk. There, he explained the situation. Theres watched the nodding and talking. She heard the urgency in Suleyman's voice, and the apologies in the clerk's.

Suleyman turned around. 'They cannot accept your other ticket in exchange, it is with a different airline. There is a flight to New York in an hour, and there is still a place on that, but you have to pay.'

'I pay, I pay', Tom impatiently stepped in. 'I need to be out of here as soon as I can. New York is a start...'

He searched for his credit card and could not find it. Theres held out his passport. 'You need that.'

'I can't find my Amex card...' his hands patted along his shirtfront and his trouser pockets. 'I need my card to pay. I need to be on this plane!'

'Tom, calm down. I pay for your flight on my card. I can get the money back when I return your other ticket, the one back to England.'

His ticket was extremely priced, and Theres hoped that her card would be flexible enough to cover the expense. When the woman swiped it through the machine, it was immediately accepted and Theres sighed in silent gratitude.

She signed the slip and put the receipt in her wallet with the card.

'I need to go.' The plane was already on the concrete, and Tom could board immediately. He was in a hurry.

He walked away from her. In his mind, he was already on the plane and on his way back. He did not hear her whisper 'I love you'. When he turned to wave, he saw her disappear, followed by Suleyman. He did not see her tears or feel her broken heart. He did not hear her world crash around her when he turned away and boarded his plane home.

CHAPTER 32

When he pushed his hand luggage into the overhead locker, Tom suddenly remembered that he had put his Amex card in his back pocket. He would let Theres know that it was safe. He looked around, and half expected her to be there, by his side. Then he remembered, she was not. This journey was his own.

He settled into his seat. He so hoped that Megan would be all right. Jenny had burst into tears so he only knew that the little one had an emergency operation to undergo, and that both Lillian and Jenny had been to the hospital. He so hoped he would be in time to help them through whatever lay ahead.

He remembered little Gretha, and thought how much she really had reminded him of Megan. Gretha had taken to Theres, and he was certain that Megan would feel comfortable with her, too. One day, he would introduce them, and his granddaughter would fall in love with his Theres, just like he had done. They would make a right pair! He could see them together, laughing and joking and carrying on. His two babes.

She would move to Detroit soon, and he would be able to see her more often. He would take his cell phone so he was always available in case of emergencies, but he would be able to spend more time with her. It would be easier, and he would find ways. He wanted to. He needed to. He needed his Theres.

He worried about getting back home in time for whatever catastrophe, and he felt the need to turn to Theres and share his feelings. But she was not where he had grown to expect her. It had not taken long for him to become so dependent on her. Was she all right now? She had not waited to wave good bye, she had walked away. And it dawned on him that he had truly left her behind. He had not waited to see what she would be doing, had just left on the drop of a hat. She would cope, he was certain, but he should have made sure she was okay.

As the plane made its way over Europe and then further, in a westerly direction, over the Atlantic Ocean, Tom settled into fitful sleep. In his dreams, Theres waved and called him to return. She laughed at him, and her laughter was not the nice, joyful outpouring of happiness that he so loved. Her laughter mocked, and he woke with a start, sweating and feeling ill. Ill with missing her. He had left her, in a strange, foreign town, to fend for herself; and then he knew that the sick feeling inside his stomach was the realization that he had not only left her, but lost her. His Theres, gone forever, and it had been his own doing. Tears welled up in his eyes once more, burning the skin of his cheek as they rolled down over his face and onto his chest. At this moment, he felt utterly alone and miserable.

CHAPTER 33

He called home as soon as he touched down in New York, but there was no answer. He knew he had to keep going, and that meant that he had to complete his journey back to his own life. In a daze, he phoned the Ambassador Hotel in Istanbul, and hoped that Theres at least would find it in her to talk to him. Maybe there was just a little spark left that would give him hope for the future, but Theres had checked out on her return from the airport. She was gone. He would have to wait before he could call her at her home in Aberdeen. He had her number there, and would find some way to call her without Lillian finding out.

Tom was lucky enough to catch a connecting flight not long after. Two hours later, he hailed a taxi to take him and his luggage straight to the local hospital. If only he could concentrate on Megan and Jenny, he would make his peace with Lillian again and maybe in time, he would be able to speak to Theres. 'Dad? Dad! What are you doing here?' Jenny's voice released him from his reverie. He turned and saw his daughter draw near him.

He stepped towards her, embracing her sincerely. 'You were so distressed, I had to come straight home. How is she?'

'O, Dad! You shouldn't have. I was so hoping you would call back, so I could explain ... Megan is fine, she is doing well, and the doctors said she will be out in a few days...'

'But you said she needed an emergency operation and you were crying, and I thought something terrible was happening. Tell me, what is going on?'

'It's not as bad as I made it sound, and Megan's operation was not even the reason for me crying. But come here, let's get off the sidewalk and find somewhere to sit.' Jenny led the way to a small park across the street, where a few benches stood empty. There, she sat down and looked at him.

'You look terrible, I am so sorry I got you this worried. And I am sorry that I spoiled your holiday. Were you enjoying it?'

Yes, he had been enjoying his holidays. He had thrived on the company of a woman only a few years older than his own daughter. What had she said? People would think their relationship dirty and sordid? He was beginning to think that himself. He should have been at home where he belonged.

To Jenny, he just nodded silently. He did not want to think of Theres, his Theres whom he still loved so deeply and whom he never would forget.

'I am sorry, Dad. Now let me tell you what went on.'

A week earlier when he and Theres had passed Vienna and spent their time in Budapest with little Gretha and her family, Megan had begun to complain about a bellyache. At first, they had thought that she might have eaten something that didn't agree with her, but then the pain had worsened and she had developed a temperature. As a precaution, they took her to the clinic. The doctor had looked at her, and sent her home with some medication to lower the temperature and make her more comfortable. Over night, Jenny had woken to hear her child cry in anguish. She had swept her up, called her mother, and they had taken Megan to the hospital. There, she was examined and a surgeon called, as the child was diagnosed with acute appendicitis.

Tom listened and pictures of Theres floated into his vision. He caught himself looking over Jenny's shoulder and waiting for Theres to appear. Always Theres. But he had left her in Istanbul. She would not come to be with him. Right now, she probably hated him.

'Dad? Are you listening?' Jenny touched his arm.

'I am sorry, I am still tired from the flight. Jet-lagged, you know. Go on.'

'As I was saying, they rushed her into theatre and started the operation. When they cut her and started on her appendix, it burst. They tried to clean her, and then they stitched her up. But over the next few days, her pain did not subside and her temperature rose again. You see, when her appendix burst, some pus had gotten into her system and the wound got infected. When you called on Thursday morning, she was on her way back into surgery for a second time.'

Megan could have died. He would have lain in the arms of Theres, making love to her, while his granddaughter, the tender life, could have died. He hated himself for his thoughts. He had to keep telling himself that it was not the fault of Theres, wonderful, lonely, precious Theres. It was his own. He had not managed to safeguard his family the way he should have done. He had put his own interest first and he hated himself for it.

Suddenly he remembered. 'Is that why you were crying?'

Jenny shook her head. She blushed slightly. 'No, I was crying because David threatened to finish with me.'

'David? Finish with you? Who is David?'

'The man I have been seeing for the past eighteen months.'

He must have mis-heard. Eighteen months? She had been seeing a man for eighteen months and he had not even been aware?

She had not told him about a new love? Why hadn't she told him? Theres had been right. He had felt hurt when she suggested that he had looked after his lot too closely, guarded them like the rooster his coop. But all along, she had been right!

'And? Did he finish with you?'

'No. We are still together. And once you are rested, I would like you to meet him. He reckons it is about time that you knew about him.'

'Does Mom know?'

'She has known for a while.'

When he eventually asked her the question, his voice changed and Jenny felt his disappointment physically: 'Why did I not know?'

'Dad, please ... I am sorry you have to find out this way.'

They sat in silence. He often had sat like this with Theres, but this silence was different. Jenny had felt that she could not trust him, had not wanted to confide in him. Hurt. More hurt. Would it ever end? O, Theres, why have I ever left you?

'Can I see the little one?'

'Of course. She will be pleased to see you, she was asking for you.'

CHAPTER 34

To all around him, Tom appeared to be the same. Inside, he was dying. He was there physically, at home with his family, but his mind was elsewhere. Lost and drifting in the torrent of his emotions, swept along, his guilt over the loss of Theres carried Tom along remorselessly.

For he had lost her. Several times, he tried to call her at home. No answer. One day, about a week after he had left her, he found her line dead. As she was ready to move to Detroit, he expected her to have gone earlier than she had said. He sent dozens of E-mails to her old account, but she did not reply. She had no need to communicate to him her anger and frustration at his desertion. Her silence punished him worse than verbal anger. He missed her more than he ever had thought possible. His light, his inspiration, his reason for living had died.

He tried to get back to his earlier routine, to remember the time before Theres. He had welcomed her with open arms, initially doubtful, but later certain, of their future together. And now ... now, faced life without her and it hurt.

Ever so slowly, he changed. His family began to notice. Jenny spoke to him about his lack of interest, then Lillian. How could he explain? He became withdrawn. Only Megan could get near, and console him during those days of utter darkness. She truly touched him. She was his only light, a faint connection to Theres as she reminded him of little Gretha. When he looked at Megan, she reminded him of the afternoon they had spent with little Gretha, and how he had planned to bring Theres and Megan together, knowing they would understand and like each other. This would never happen now.

He had drunk from the cup of true love, and discarded it on the basis of one tearful phone call. He wished he had never found out about Megan's operation, had never phoned home that day.

He tried to make love with Lillian, but that was just mechanical. They had nothing to say to each other, he had nothing to say to her, and nothing left to give. One day, he asked her permission to move out. She was not astounded, and her hurt did not seem as deep as his. He packed some of his things into a suitcase, filled a few boxes with his favorite books, and loaded them into his pick-up.

When Megan ran out to stop him from leaving, he told her that he needed to go away, on a long holiday, but that she could always call him on his cellular phone. He got in his vehicle and drove off. He did not look back. Nothing could have made him stop.

He drove on and on, occasionally stopping to refill the pick-up or to stretch his legs, till he found himself drifting along the Mexican border. In a motel, he booked a room for a few nights. Unsure where he was going, he pondered his options.

For two nights and days, he slept, drank, and slept some more. On the third day, he showered, changed into clean clothes, and got back into his pick-up to return to Appalachia.

He had lost Theres, but he did not want to lose Megan or Jenny as well. He could not go back to Lillian, but he still needed to be close to his girls. In the end, he took a small apartment near Megan's school so he could see her some afternoons. His little girl took his absence from the old house in her stride, and adapted to his new surroundings as only children can.

He bought a new PC and checked his old Hotmail account, just in case Theres had written to him. There was no message from her. Slowly, he read through all the letters that she had written to him in the months before he had gone to Aberdeen. He printed them all out, and read and re-read them time and time again. Some days, the sun would set and he would sit by the window, staring out and wondering what could have been. Sometimes, he cried.

In one of her letters, she described the new job she had found in Detroit and the name of the new company. He got their phone number from the white pages and rang. The receptionist pretended never to have heard of Theres, and he hung up. The last connection seemed lost.

Often, Jenny would come and visit. She saw him suffer, and sink deeper and deeper into depression. She wanted to help and would listen to him talk, a companion at times when there were no words. Most of the time though, there was silence, interrupted by the odd sigh. She saw him turn into himself, and felt utterly helpless.

Sometimes, she brought Megan. Something close to happiness would come back into his life. She would tell of her adventures at school or her outings with her mom, spent hours just talking to him about anything that came into her head, the patter of an innocent child. Children and Theres. Ever so often, David came along as well. They had talked of marriage and Jenny hoped for her father's approval. David was happy, though, to wait till Tom felt better. A happy wedding could not be as long as the father of the bride was in Tom's state. David would wait for Jenny, till the right time.

At night, Tom lay sleepless and longed for her body beside him. She had opened him to pleasures he had only dreamt of before, had taken him out of himself, and now he was in a worse state than ever. Worse, because he had tasted what could have been. Knowing nobody was to blame but him, he suffered.

One afternoon, Jenny found him by his window, tears in his eyes. He watched life outside pass by, but did not see. Her heart went out to him and she crouched by his side, hugging and holding him in her arms.

'Dad.'

He sobbed, and she looked for tissues.

'I can't live like this any longer.'

'Dad, you frighten me when you speak like this!'

He turned towards her and for the first time in weeks, he saw her.

'Jenny, help me!'

The feeling inside made her strong and she pulled a chair close to him. She held his hand while he needed her there. She knew he finally wanted to talk.

'Whatever I can do for you, I will. O Dad, I don't want to see you like this! It is breaking my heart, and Mom's. We want you back the way you were. Please let me help!'

A sigh breathed from deep inside his soul.

'Jenny, dear, it will never be like before. But I need your help. I need to find someone.'

His eyes pleaded and she remained silent, hoping he would open up to her.

'I need you to listen to what I have to say. I beg of you not to judge me harshly for what I have done…'

'Dad, just tell me.' Seeing him suffer had made her eyes water. ' I will sit here and listen to whatever you have to say. It can't be as bad as you think it is. You are not a bad person, I can't think what you could have done to get yourself into this state…'

Another sigh and a short silence followed. He held her hand and remembered the happy times with Theres, sitting in silence and holding on to her. He began.

'I have ruined everything.' And then the banks of the river broke and it all tumbled out.

'It started some time in January. You know I have been taking an increased interest in the computer, and with you and your Mom working, I had a lot of time on my hands.'

Jenny felt him climb out of the depths of his despair with every word, and she saw his strength slowly return.

'One day, I decided to ... I don't know how to say this ... find myself a woman friend. You know, like a penfriend? A lady to talk to during the day, on the Internet.'

He threw Jenny a glance to gauge her reaction. But the girl urged him to continue.

"That is how I met Theres. The moment I came across her, I knew she was so special.'

Tom stood up and began to pace the tiny room. Jenny's eyes followed him, he had her attention and she did not want him to stop.

'At first, it was just emails. We wrote to each other daily, sometimes even more often. Then, we met online in a chatroom and when she asked whether she could phone me, I gave her my number. You know, she knew about you and your Mom. There were no secrets between us. She is only two years older than you are, and I was so flattered that she should even want to know me. She's got a good career, so she was not after money or anything like that. She liked me. She was on the brink of taking a new job in Detroit. She is from Scotland, that is where she called me from. One day, she suggested meeting. Remember when I went traveling in Europe? I went to meet her.'

Tom stopped again. Jenny had turned away from him, and now she looked out the window.

'As soon as I met her and we spent time together, I knew I loved her. Don't get me wrong, I loved your Mom and in a way I still do. But Theres ... she was more than that. She was life to me. She made me feel so good inside. She never needed me, like Lillian always did. She chose to be with me and I honestly believed there would be a future for us. And then I called home, just to make sure you all were okay. You know the rest.'

And still, Jenny sat and looked outside. He revealed the emptiness he had felt, filled only by herself and Megan, and how his love for Lillian had turned into mutual understanding and concern for the children. Suddenly, there had been Theres. Theres, who had a career and a husband, but who was so full of life and so willing to share with him. Theres, who had made him look forward to every new day, who had made waiting for her letters so deliciously pleasurable.

He felt awkward telling his daughter about his physical needs and desires, but she understood. She sat and listened, while he told her about the train journey to London, and then the Orient Express.

He told her about Little Gretha and Budapest. Finally, he told her about the fateful day in Istanbul, when he left Theres.

'I have regretted this ever since. I have nightmares about leaving her behind. Sometimes, she laughs and smirks at me for my weaknesses. Once I have seen her killed, lying in a pool of blood and screaming. Jenny, o Jenny ... what have I done?'

Jenny sat back and tried to take it all in. Her mother had wondered about another woman in Toms' life, but she never would have expected anything like this. He was right, there was no going back. Lillian was beginning to live happily by herself, realizing that she did not really need Tom to make her life whole. Jenny began to reply. No matter how she felt about her father's actions, his deceit and the effects on all the family, she had to assure that he would keep on talking and get out of his depression. That she owed him as his daughter.

'Whatever you have done is done. I can't condone the secrecy and the lies you told us. The point is - what are you going to do now?'

Tom shrugged.

'I have tried to get in touch with her, ever since I came back. But her phone in Aberdeen was cut off, at her new office they tell me they don't know of her, I don't know where else to look. What can I do?'

She looked into his eyes and saw his need for her help. He relied on her for his salvation.

'Her letters, do you still have them? Is there anything in her letters? Any clue about her family maybe?'

'I have looked at her letters, time and time again. I know the name of her mother, and that she lives in the South of Germany, I know where she was born, but no more. These things had never been important to us, we were to be together forever. Till I left her.'

'Can I see her letters? Maybe I can find a clue?'

'Sure.'

Tom pointed to a box on a low shelf behind him.

'They are all in there. Some of them are quite explicit, please don't think that all this was just an old man's second youth and she was just a cheap, loose woman. I loved her, I still do, and I need her back.'

'Don't worry, Dad. I will make my mind up about her when I meet her.'

Jenny smiled. At last, her father had talked. She had worried so. Her mother did not really want him back, she had found her own life, her own freedom. Now, she would make sure her father found his happiness. Whether he truly deserved it, she was as yet unsure. Her head whirled after his revelations, but she struggled and focused on the immediate task.

Theres was so near to her in age but yet so ageless that her father could have fallen for her. She had everything, a husband, a career, yet she risked it for a man more than twenty years her senior, set in his ways, graying and growing older, with nothing more to offer than what was left of himself.

Theres' letters were a revelation to Jenny. She was getting to know this person, how Theres would have felt that day in August, when Tom left her in Istanbul. She would have felt the same. And Jenny felt sorry for her, sorry for her father's reaction to her crying on the phone, and sorry for his exceptional concern for his brood. She hoped she could help him find her, that they were not too late. She wanted to give him hope but didn't dare. After all, they could fail to find Theres, and he truly might have lost her.

She took paper and some pencils to take notes while she was reading. She found the name of Theres' parents, and an indication of where in Germany they lived.

'Dad, get on the Internet, and we see what we can find out!'

With new vigor and suddenly wide awake, Tom logged on. Jenny would help him find his Theres, and all would be well.

CHAPTER 35

Jenny was good with the computer, used to getting the best information out of the Internet. They found a site for the German Telecom, but there was no facility to search for all occurrences of any surname nationwide.

'Dad, do you know anything about where her parents lived? We need to narrow it down to a region or district or something.'

She looked at him, willing him to remember anything. He thought and then he remembered the castle in Rumania.

'King Carol. He was King of Rumania in the Nineteenth Century. His family is from the same area where her parents live. I remember because she once said that the Swabians were less boisterous about getting their royalty than the Bavarians, and then we went to see this castle in Rumania as part of the trip, and Carol who came from Swabia had built it. Can you search for him?'

It didn't take long before she had found out that Carol had been a member of the Hohenzollern-Sigmaringen line. Both these names were those of small towns in southern Germany. Jenny returned to the web page of the Telecom and entered name and area information.

'Look, we are on the right track - they still are there. Although, they are ex-directory. Dead end for now.'

Jenny went back to Theres' letters. She saw how animated her father had become when she got him involved in the search for Theres, and how he now sat back in his chair, looking out the window. She had to keep trying, and if she could not help, they would have to seek help elsewhere.

'I still love her, you know. Do you think she might have me back?'

He worried and feared that he had lost her, and there would be no returning to the easy togetherness. Maybe he didn't even have the right to ask her back, should he ever find her again. For now, he had hope and his memories.

'She seems to genuinely love you. Her letters are so warm and caring, no wonder you fell in love with her... and she looks so beautiful!'

Tom looked at the photograph Jenny had found amongst the letters. It showed Theres the way he remembered her best, with that lovely smile radiating like the sun. So beautiful...

'Do you really think that? Jenny, I am so glad you don't damn me for cheating on your mother. I thought when I told you about that I might lose you as well. That is what I always was so intensely worried about. But I needed to tell you so badly, I know if anybody can help me, then it is you.'

'Mom is getting on fine, you know. She is taking your absence a lot better than you give her credit for. She is strong and still full of energy. You worry too much about us. And see where it got you to!'

She immersed herself in the letters again.

'Did you ever talk about Mom or Ben?'

Tom thought. Lillian and Ben had somehow always been with them, if not physically, then in their minds. He knew that Theres' coming to the States was to get away from Ben, that she had wanted to leave long before they had met. He never had been that sure about Lillian. He always had believed that Lillian could not cope without him, that as her husband, his duty was to look after her. Her and Jenny and Megan. David now looked after Jenny and Megan, and Lillian seemed to do fine without him. He was superfluous to their needs. He wanted Theres, who would never need him, but would permit him to be with her. He hoped against all hope that...

'We talked about your Mom and Ben. But not much.'

Jenny concentrated on the letters. When she came across a collection of jokes, she laughed and Tom looked at her.

'Funny, these jokes.' And then she noticed the names of other recipients of the same email.

'Dad?'

'Yes, Jenny?'

'Do you still operate this Hotmail account?'

'I do. Why?'

'When is the last time you checked it?'

'Two days ago. I often check to see whether she might not have written to me after all. Any sign from her would be better than her silence, even if it was an angry letter!'

'And you saved her letters, did you?'

'Jenny? What is it?'

'Did you?'

'Yes, I did. They are the only thing that connects me to her still.'

'Show me.'

So they went back to the computer, and he logged into his Hotmail account. A few clicks, and he had the whole list of Theres' emails in front of Jenny.

Jenny was only interested in the one email that contained the jokes. She opened it and in the address line, there were the names of all Theres' friends who had received the same note. Among them was 'mum'. Jenny double-clicked on this addressee and an email address appeared. She had found a way to Theres' family, and therefore Theres.

CHAPTER 36

It had been that easy, it had been there all the time. The email address had been with him for over a year. If it hadn't been for Jenny, he would never have known. He was glad he had taken his daughter into his confidence and chided himself for not having done so sooner. He had wasted so much valuable time!

Jenny showed him how to save the address so he could not lose it again. He needed to make sure it was there, maybe the last little link he had to Theres.

'Are you going to write to her?' Jenny had asked.

'I don't know what to say', he had replied. He wanted to tell her mother all the worry he had in his heart, his fear of never seeing Theres again, and apologize for all the hurt he had caused. Her mother might not even know about him, so maybe he should just take it easy.

Jenny sensed his indecision.

'Come on, Dad. You can't give up now. Shall we do this together?'

Tom smiled. 'I would like that.'

They discussed his first letter to Theres' mother Margit over a glass of wine. Since leaving Theres in Istanbul, he had not opened a bottle of white wine himself. He felt better already, as though he expected her to call any moment now. A weight had been lifted, his life began to look up. He had hope.

CHAPTER 37

In the end, they decided on the following short note to Margit:

Dear Margit.

I would like to get in touch with Theres but I don't know where she is. Please, could you let me have her email address or get her to write to me here at mine? I would very much appreciate this.

Thanking you kindly,

Tom.

When Jenny hit the 'send' button, Tom started to shake.

'No way back now. I hope you said your prayers for me, Jenny.' He stood behind her, watching the computer screen, holding his daughter and hoping for the best.

Tom waited for several days, going through heaven and hell. Every day, he checked his Inbox several times, and he prayed. At times, he would sit in front of the screen, egging it on to produce a letter from Theres. More than a week later, Margit replied:

Tom -

Theres does not want to write to you. Sorry.

Margit

He waited to show Jenny. His mood had changed again, he had spiraled back into the depth of depression. Jenny came and saw he had cried, the traces of his tears still visible. She felt so sorry for him, and decided to write a letter to Margit herself.

'Dear Margit

Thank you so much for replying to my Dad's email.

Dad is devastated, but deep down in his heart he understands your daughter's decision.

I didn't know about Theres till Dad told me on the day we sent you his email. For the past year, Dad has been very depressed and eventually, he had to take someone into his confidence. That someone was me. I only know Theres from her letters that Dad kept. All I can say is that he is sorry for the pain he must have caused her. Even though I understand Theres not wanting to speak to him again, I believe she should know what he is going through and that he truly loves her. I feel a little responsible for what happened that day in Istanbul, as it was my childish behavior that made Dad leave Theres, so I hope you can find it in you to help, just as I did.

Even if your daughter does not want to communicate with Dad, maybe she would write to me. Please, help us.

Jenny'

Margit replied. She promised to speak with Theres again and would be in touch. She did not and could not promise anything more than that. Jenny reassured her father. This was a good sign. He needed to be positive.

Tom went back to Lillian and asked for a divorce. He expected her to be upset, to scream and shout. Instead, she only looked at him without emotion, then gave him the business card of her own solicitor. She had already sought legal advice. Their separation would be harmonious. She would keep the house and garden for herself and Jenny, he would sell the second car and take the money. Neither foresaw any problems.

He still looked at Theres' letters, and missed her more than ever. Sometimes, he woke up at night, and imagined her body next to his. He needed her so badly. At Christmas, he sent Margit an Internet card and got one in return. Margit did not seem angry, and he hoped he could rely on her help to speak to Theres.

In January, Jenny and David got married. Both families and a few friends celebrated. Megan was a proud and beautiful bridesmaid. She adored David, and he would look after her like a father should. He also would look after Jenny and Tom was content. Lillian spoke to him like to an old friend. Jenny had confessed to her about Theres. After initial anger and fury, Lillian had come to terms with the idea that Tom was in love with another woman. In a sense, she pitied him. The day of the wedding had been pleasurable enough. When Jenny and

David drove off on their honeymoon, Tom and Lillian had waved them off together.

It was the middle of March, when Tom received another email from Margit.

Dear Tom,

I am sorry you had to wait this long for my letter. Theres still does not want to speak to you, but I think there are things you should know. Please come to Germany during the second week in August. I can collect you from Stuttgart airport.

Margit

Overjoyed, he printed this email off and read it and read it again. Then he phoned Jenny and she came round. Together, they booked his tickets there and then, on the Internet. He would get there on a Wednesday, early afternoon, and he wondered if Theres would be at her Mother's house or if she would even pick him up herself. The old zest returned, and he was ready to go. By the time he got there, it would be nearly twenty-four months since Istanbul. He could not imagine her reaction on seeing him. There could be tears, shouting, anger, and even arguments. How would he react when he saw her again? Deep in his heart, he knew they had never been apart, that they had been joined forever in their spirits.

He prayed that she would hear him out.

CHAPTER 38

Still not knowing whom to expect at Stuttgart, Tom was nervous when Jenny accompanied him to the airport. He sat in the car, silent, before words began to bubble out as from an uncorked bottle. She probed to find out his expectations, but all he could think about was seeing Theres once more. Jenny wondered about his obsession for the younger woman, but they had talked. Talked about Theres and the changes she had brought about in his life. Talked about his love for her, so much stronger than any other before. That her mother had not been the love of her father's life, Jenny comprehended with difficulty, but his account of the beautiful, special and lovely Theres caught her imagination, and she looked forward to meeting her, too.

She had spoken to Lillian about her feelings, and Lillian had consoled her daughter. She and Tom had had a good life together, but she had known he was not as happy as he could have been. She had wondered, but had never spoken, of her fear of him walking away. Now that he had left, she strangely felt relieved. She still had a purpose and a new spring in her step. Maybe one day, there would be a new love for her, and she was beginning to see the world around her in a new light. Lillian was neither angry nor sad, and had wished him well, though she had not spoken to Tom herself. She avoided him whenever possible, not wanting to stir emotions.

From his local airport, Tom flew via New York and was reminded of his last journey through this airport and all the changes that had taken place since. He so hoped to put things right. For the onward journey to Frankfurt, he managed to secure a seat by himself, so he would not be forced to talk to anybody. He had brought a book, 'Great Expectations', that he had read many times, as it brought Theres' spirit back to him. Memories. The last night on the Orient Express, her voice and the way her body felt, cradled into him when she finally fell asleep and he had put her to bed. He had great expectations himself. He tried hard to curb them, to not expect too much, to not be disappointed. He was painfully aware that with every second, the plane brought him closer to his Theres.

In Frankfurt, he struggled to catch his flight-connection to Stuttgart. His palms sweated, his stomach fluttered and somersaulted. A young man, who looked like a student but turned out to be a teacher on holidays, sat next to him and struck up a conversation. Tom remembered that Theres' mother was a teacher, that she might be there to collect him, as she, too, would be on holiday. The flight passed in a daze. He abstained from food and beverages. He yearned for a large Scotch, but doubted that would solve his problems.

His luggage made the journey with him. He collected his bag, made his way through the exit doors, and began looking for a familiar face. He could not see Theres, but he was not certain she was supposed to be there. He began to worry that there might not be anybody to collect him, when he heard a voice call his name.

He found himself facing a petite woman, about his own age. He stood opposite Margit, as svelte as her daughter was voluptuous.

They shook hands formally. She seemed tense, and he was still nervous. But the thought elevated him that he had come one step closer to Theres. Margit had the same sparkling eyes as Theres, but she had not the gift of Theres' smile. Did her smile still sparkle the same way that had enwebbed and aroused him so much in the past? Or had hurt taken it away?

'I thought we go and have a chat before we decide what to do next. There are one or two things I want to clear up first.'

Tom nodded. She was in charge - as Theres had been - and he had to go along. Her English was passable, with a strong German accent. In Margit's voice were traces of Theres' inflection, but it rang not as melodic. He had to stop making these comparisons. They did not get him any further towards his love and dreams.

They found a coffee shop and sat down. Margit ordered a mineral water for herself, and some coffee for Tom. When it came, his hands shook so much so he could not lift his cup. Instead, he held on to it, hoping Margit would not notice his edginess.

'I wanted to meet you for a while', she said at last. 'When your first email came, I spoke to Theres and she told me all about you. Before then, all I had was your name and that was not enough to find you.'

'It took me some time to find you. My daughter, Jenny, found your email address amongst something that Theres had sent me, some jokes that she had forwarded to you and me.'

'Yes, I had thought of that, but I had deleted her messages and saved things like the jokes elsewhere. Anyway, let us not talk about this. There are two things I want to know. First, why are you here?'

Tom swallowed hard. He was not prepared for an investigation of his motives, but he responded immediately.

'I love Theres and I want to find out whether she still cares enough about me to forget Istanbul.'

'You left her there. It was clear to her that you would never love her enough to stay with her. She says your family would always get in the way. She needs someone who will always put her first, and she knew that you weren't this person.'

Tom's face burned. His eyes stung. Margit watched him closely.

'I am so sorry.... ', was all he could say.

Margit's face set. He could not make out whether she really would help him to speak to Theres, or whether she would destroy him completely by leaving him stranded at the airport. Maybe he should not have come, but this was the only way that might lead him back to Theres.

'You are married.'

He looked up from his coffee cup, and into her face.

'Not for much longer. I could not stand the deceit any more and moved out over a year ago. I had become very depressed and needed time to myself. That is when I not only realized that I need Theres and that I had treated her despicably, but when I finally acted.'

When he added 'I love her so much', it was like his soul shouted out in desperation, and Margit saw his distress at his own actions, when he had made a rash decision that had cost him her daughter.

'You know, my husband thinks I am mad for getting involved. Theres does not know where I am right now - and who I am with - and he promised not to tell her. I know she still deeply cares about you, she has every reason to. But she believes that you never will truly love her, that your own daughter and granddaughter will always 'call the shots', so to speak...'

'But...' he began. Margit lifted her hands.

'Please, let me speak.'

Tom tried to lift his cup, but his hands shook, and he spilled coffee into the saucer. He apologized and leant back in his seat. He would listen to whatever she had to say, he deserved her reproach.

'Maybe things have changed in your life, but you will have to convince Theres about that, not me. Her life has changed as well. After she came back, she gave up on the job in Detroit, she never went. She got a transfer with her own company to Texas. She has been in Houston ever since. Ben went with her for a while, but they separated soon after. Now, she still works there. She is alone with the baby...'

'Theres has a child?' Tom looked up, stunned. Theres must have gone back to the clinic after all. Maybe she had tried to get things back on track with Ben, only to find out that it would not, could not work. Maybe there was hope.

Margit examined his face closely. Then she got her handbag and took out a photograph. Theres and her child.

'She has a little boy. He is nearly fifteen months old now. A wonderful little fellow, a little miracle. See for yourself.'

She pushed the picture across to Tom who greedily held it up to see it close. Theres smiled back at him, as he remembered her. The child in her arms looked so much like her, he immediately recognized him as the fruit of her womb. Her mouth and her nose. Her green eyes. The baby's darker eyes, almost brown, enormously deep. He loved her child as much as he loved her. If she would let him.

'You can keep that picture if you like. I think you should have it.'

Tom nodded. He looked at Theres and her baby, and the ache inside became physical. He should have been with her, he should never have left her.

Margit stood up and motioned him to follow.

'I think it is time to go. We have a journey of slightly over an hour, and I want to miss the afternoon traffic.'

'Where are we going?' Tom inquired.

'O, didn't I tell you? I do apologize! I am going to take you back to our place. Theres and the baby are staying with us for a month. I want you to see her.'

Still holding on to the photograph, Tom grabbed his case, and they made their way to Margit's car.

He could not speak for a long while, and they set off in mutual silence. Margit wanted to talk, but felt the weight of his silence. She would not and could not inflict any more news on him. The news of the baby had surprised him. Margit expected her daughter to be angry with her for interfering, but Tom and Theres had issues to discuss, and both had suffered during the two years since Istanbul. Margit was determined to give them their chance.

It was Tom who broke the silence.

'Why are you doing this? Even your own husband does think you should not get involved?'

Margit glanced at him briefly before concentrating on the busy road ahead.

'I don't know what Theres has told you about our relationship, but she still has not forgiven me that I was not there for her when she was little. I believe you have a right to know what happened after you left her in Istanbul, a right to know about the baby and all the rest of it.

She may not be willing to talk to you, but I want you to have the chance to say your piece. In a way, I want to make it up to her.'

She fell silent, overtaking a line of lorries, then continued.

'So much happened in the last two years, and you have been the catalyst to most. You need to know the effect you had on her life. I was unsure of what you wanted of her, whether you even were free to talk about a future together with her. She is here for a month, so that we can have time with our grandson, before she goes back to Texas. A good opportunity for you as well, don't you think?'

'Yes', he agreed, ' and I am glad of it. Tell me, is she well?'

'You will find her changed, but I believe that is due to her responsibilities as a mother. A single working mother at that. In the end, she still is Theres, and that will never change. There are no limits to what she can and will do. But I suppose you know that. She is very special, but I don't need to tell you that!'

Again, Tom sank into silence. He looked at the photograph, and his eyes concentrated on the child in her arms.

'What is the boy's name?'

'Theres decided to call him after his father. Even though they were not together any longer, there still should be a memory. She felt this was the right thing to do.'

Theres and little Ben. He would love them. Their life would be complete together. As long as Theres would come back to him.

'Did you have a good journey?' Margit asked. He talked about traveling, and small talk continued till she turned her car off the motorway, and into the countryside of the Swabian Alps. Rich, dark forests flanked the road, winding its way steeply up and up till they reached a plateau, and he saw fields ready for the onslaught of a late harvest. Margit turned left once more, on a single-track thoroughfare that meandered through one village after another.

Tom could make out farm buildings, large stable doors, cows tied up inside, chewing freshly cut grass. Flowers and vegetables fought for attention in the gardens. Tom began to relax, enveloped in loveliness and calm.

'Theres will be out, but I tell you where you can find her. I think you better come in first and freshen up a little. The baby will be there, so you can meet the boy.'

Margit pulled into the drive of a large stone house in the center of the village. Tom got out, and was greeted immediately by a gray cat, winding around his legs, purring loudly.

'I hope you don't mind the cats, there are three of them', Margit explained.

Tom smiled, gently moved away from the cat that followed close behind, as they entered the house.

The moment he entered, happy memories confronted him. Opposite the entrance hung a portrait of Theres. He gasped involuntarily, and Margit followed his eyes.

'Paris, yes?'

'Yes, that was a happy day.'

His eyes could not let go of the picture.

'You better come along now', Margit urged. 'This is the guestroom. Theres is staying upstairs, so please, have a shower, there are towels and things, and I go and find my husband. When you are done, please come upstairs.'

Tom did as he was bid. The guestroom was large and generously furnished. When he sat on the bed, another large cat, this one black, jumped up in surprise and skittled out of the room on bent legs. He closed the door and entered the bathroom on the far side. Here was a shower, a sink and a toilet. If Theres did not want him, he could stay in this mini-apartment till he caught the next plane back to ... not home ... just ... his life. An empty life without her.

The water was hot, and he felt refreshed, walking up the stairs to the first floor. He heard a baby cooing and followed the sound. Margit sat on the floor in a large room, lined with books from floor to ceiling along two walls. On the third, immediately to his left, a large TV and stereo system imposed. A picture window faced from the remaining wall out to the garden and an orchard beyond.

Margit looked up when she heard him approach. She smiled and turned to the baby, saying 'look who it is!' as though the little boy would know him already.

Tom sank down on the floor next to them, and stretched his arms out to the boy, holding him up high, then hugging him close to his chest. The baby raised his arms and touched Tom's face.

'Hello, little Ben', he smiled at him.

'Ben? Why do you call him Ben?' Margit said in surprise.

'Didn't you say Theres called him after his father?' Tom returned her question.

'We call him TJ. His name is Thomas Jack. After his father. Didn't you know?'

When the true meaning of her words hit Tom, tears started. Looking at the photograph, he should have recognized not only

Theres, but also himself. He should have known that there was more to Margit's words, that this little boy was why she felt he needed to speak to Theres. This little boy. His son.

CHAPTER 39

'Where is he?' Peter asked Margit when he returned from the shops ten minutes later.

'He didn't know about the baby, I was right. It has come as quite a shock to him. He is in the front room, with TJ.'

Margit had been embarrassed by Tom's emotional outburst. He had hugged the baby, his son, close to his chest again and again, rocking gently and struggling to fathom the depths of his feelings and despair over lost time. His world had changed yet again. Theres, once again, had changed his world. Until now, he had not known to what extent she had changed things. Her baby, his son, in his arms, looking at him, smiling and touching him gently, wiping at his tears. Warmth and love took over. Slowly, Tom regained strength and control over his heart. He needed to talk to Theres more than ever now, she could not deny hearing him out. He had fathered her child, she had given him a son.

Whispering drew him outside on the landing, and he still held the boy close when he went out to greet Peter.

'I have to apologize, I did not know about the baby. My son.' The man shook his hand and grinned awkwardly. He said something in German and Margit had to translate.

'Peter does not speak your language. He thinks you should go and see Theres now. I will take the boy.'

Margit took the baby from a reluctant Tom and led him back down and out at the front door. There, she motioned him to turn left.

'If you walk along the road, you will come to a turn to the right. Take that and it will lead you up the hill. Halfway on your left, you will see the horses. That is where Theres will be.'

Before she closed the door, she added: 'Good luck' and left him alone in the street.

Over the past few months, Tom had envisioned meeting Theres, but he had never thought of a setting like this for their reunion. He had never thought of a son. He remembered when he told her that he would never force her to have a child. She would be enough for him. Now, there was so much more.

Haltingly, then with increasing confidence, he stepped along the empty, late afternoon village road, found the turning to his right and started up the hill. He saw the horses on his left. Approaching, he heard her laughter. Her voice stopped him in mid-stride, and he had to control the onset of nerves fluttering. His palms sweated. His face flushed. So close, so close to her!

Still, he could not see her, and he walked nearer to the jumble of buildings. She had once told him about her friend with the horses, and the strange place where she felt so at ease. Her friend, after an accident as a teenager, gave up conventional work, and ferried paying guests around in his horse-drawn carriages. This must be the place.

As he approached the gates of the ranch, a large dog snarled from a kennel, and Tom looked to make sure that the dog could not get at him. The black thing snarled again, but he entered the enclosure and stood in a yard, with stables to his right and farm machinery scattered around.

He walked along farther, to an area where he had seen the horses from the road. And then he saw her.

Of dozen horses and ponies, the most impressive stood in the center of the meadow, head bowed, nibbling grass. A tall, sturdy, gray-coated animal. The horse did not move. On his back stood, feet on the horse's wide midriff, Theres, with arms outstretched and face towards the mellow evening sun.

Warmth and light suffused the scene. He only saw her outline, and shaded his eyes with his hand. She wore dungarees and a T-shirt. Her body had more defined curves, and her waist seemed smaller than Tom remembered. His throat burned. His heart ached. He never would forget.

He watched. So like a dream, far away, and yet so real. Her hair was longer, tied back in a ponytail. He remembered her by the sea, windswept and erotic. Now she stood on the back of a horse, saluting the Goddess of the Sun, kissed and embraced by the still, warm air.

His love went out to her. He wanted to hold her close to him, kiss her gently like the sun was kissing her, warm and passionate, and at the same time, he was reluctant to break the spell. Tom wanted this moment to last, needed for it to be there in the future. The horse grazed patiently, inching forward, shifting slowly from one hefty leg to the other, surrounded by smaller horses and ponies. He must not startle them. She might fall off.

'Hallo?'

He turned, astonished, and found himself face to face with an enormous giant of a man, burnt dark reddish brown. When he moved closer, Tom saw he had one crippled foot, and knew this must be her friend from long ago.

'Hello', Tom replied. Then he gestured in the direction of Theres, and said: 'I have come to speak to her.'

The giant nodded and called over to Theres in German. Theres turned. She looked at him. Their eyes met. Her face lost the warm smile, and she lowered herself onto the back of the horse. She jostled the steed to a step, glided down, and landed carefully on her own two feet.

Tom did not move. He waited for her to come to him.

She stood in front of him and they looked at each other. They drank each other in, and locked eyes.

The giant put his hand protectively on her shoulder.

'Okay?' he asked.

Her reply must have soothed his fears, as he turned and left. Tom watched him go.

'Tom', she whispered.

'Yes, dear', he replied.

'What are you doing here?' Her question did not reproach him. She wanted to know, expected a straight-forward answer.

'I want to talk to you.'

'How did you know where to find me?'

'Your mother...'

'You have met...?'

'TJ?'

And when she nodded, he added 'Yes.'

Insects thrummed. Horses stomped. Tails swished. Her eyes sparkled. He wanted to hold her.

Theres must have felt the same. Suddenly, they clutched at each other like two people lost in a flood, swept away by the torrents of their lives.

'Can we talk, Theres?'

She moved away. 'Yes, I think we should. But not here. Let us go somewhere else.'

She led the way back to her parents' house in silence. There, she took the baby, fed and changed in their absence, and together they strapped TJ into his seat in her rental car. They drove off. In the back, the little boy played and cooed and told the story of his feet, energetically kicking. Tom turned and the little fellow appreciated the attention.

Their journey took no more than twenty minutes, leading along fields and forests. Theres stopped and they got out. She let Tom carry the baby in its seat. She grabbed a blanket and small bag for the boy.

'Not far', she said.

She led Tom along a path into the trees. Little flies congregated and followed. Suddenly, the trees gave way. Tom found himself looking out over the lake, with Switzerland at the far shore, and Austria hidden in the haze to his left. They found a bench and sat.

From a road below, they could hear the hum of cars and an occasional horn. A train rolled past in the distance. Church bells chimed peacefully for ev'n song. Little white triangles skimmed over the water. A big dark ferry silently glided across.

They sat and gathered their courage to speak.

CHAPTER 40

With the setting of the sun came a chill that crept from the lake and goose-pimpled them. Theres covered the baby, asleep in its blanket. She looked at Tom, sitting next to her, looking out over the silent lake.

'There are more blankets in the boot of the car.'

'If you give me the key, I will get them.'

He walked away. Theres did not move. When he returned, she sat the way he had left her. Without a further word, she took one of the blankets and wrapped herself into it. He did the same.

'As you have found me, I think you should talk first.'

As earlier, there was no reproach, no accusation, just an invitation. Tom knew she would listen.

'First, let me assure you that I am so sorry for leaving you the way I did. I can't forgive myself and I won't ask for your forgiveness.'

Theres did not react, and he continued.

'At the time, I thought they needed me. I believed Megan to be seriously ill and I felt that I had betrayed her and Jenny as well as Lillian by being with you. By being so happy with you. There I was, making love to you, and my little girl dying. The moment I got on that plane and you left without even looking back, I knew I had lost you. The moment I got on that plane, I missed you.'

His voice failed, his lower lip quivered. He fought to hold back tears. He had to make the most of his time while she listened.

'I have loved you all my life, I still do. But at the time, things were out of perspective, out of focus. I felt responsible for the girls and I had neglected them. I had been selfish. I realized that and my whole world crashed down around me. I should not have left the way I did, I know that. I tried to write to you but you never replied. I had lost you for good. In the end, I moved out. If I want anybody in my life, it is you. And now there is TJ, but I didn't know about him till earlier today. I wish you had told me, I would have been there for you!'

She looked at him, crying soundlessly. Tears glistened on her cheek in the soft light.

'I told you before, I would never have done anything to make you choose. You did that all by yourself. And you did not choose me. Why should I believe you now when you tell me that you want me back? We don't need you!'

'I love you.'

'That is not enough any longer. You made your point clear. You wanted to be with Megan and Jenny, not with me. All the things you had told me had been nothing but lies. All the promises you made ... the future together ... our dreams ... meant nothing to you when Jenny cried for help. I wish you hadn't come!'

At her outburst, the baby woke and started crying. She stood up and took the boy into her arms, wrapping him in her blanket and his, bouncing him gently up and down.

Tom came up behind her and held her arms. She stood there with the baby, and he smelled her hair as he had done so many times before.

'I never wanted to be anything but your stepping stone to a brighter future. I have failed in that. I have been a millstone and it has been on my conscience ever since. I have hurt you. Theres, if there is a chance that you might love me again one day, and be with me, I take that chance. But tell me, look at me and tell me that you don't love me. That there is not even a little spark left of your old feelings for me. I will go away and leave you alone. I will never bother you again, I will not just turn up on your doorstep uninvited. Don't say that my love for you is not enough. It will be - if you only let it. Please ... Theres?'

She shook her head.

'Theres, I beg of you, think about it. I will be whatever you want me to be. Just allow me to be part of your life. Your life and TJ's. You must still feel something for me, you named your son, our son, after me. Theres, please...'

His voice had grown intense. He needed her to forgive him, he did not want to leave without her promise to think about a new beginning. Together. For good.

'You are not free to be what I would like you to be.'

'My love, I am free to be whatever you want me to be. Jenny knows I am here, she knows all about you and even wants to meet you. She got married just over six months ago, she is not my responsibility any more. Neither is Megan. I always will be her grandfather, but she now has a proper father who dotes on her and spoils her. My divorce is nearly through, I have no longer responsibility for Lillian. I am free. Free for you and TJ.'

Still, she had not turned. Beneath his hands, he sensed her tension, and the intensity of her emotions.

'Can you promise me that when either of them are calling on you, that you will consider me first? That you won't just pack your bags and leave me again?'

He turned her to face him, and embraced her and held her as close as possible with the baby between them.

'I will never leave you like I did in Istanbul. Theres, I offer you myself and my eternal love. I am still 23 years older than you, I turned gray since I lost you, and you know what I am like. If you have me, please, Theres, it is all yours. That, and whatever else I can give you.'

'I will think about it.' Her face was set in indignation.

She freed herself from his hold and sat down again, covering herself in the blanket. Tom sat beside her, looking out over the lake and watching the lights of Switzerland sparkle on the opposite shore.

'We can't have been all that far away from this place where we had our midnight picnic, can we?'

'No'.

For the first time, she smiled. 'I actually went back there and found the spot. For some reason I thought I might feel so much closer to you there, but you weren't there and the moment was lost.'

'O, Theres, I should have been with you and the little one. In my thoughts I so often was with you.'

'I knew you would find me. One day.' Her voice was that of a child's and he knew she still loved him. His dreams of being with her would come true. Better, he had a son.

Silence descended and she moved closer up against him. He put his arm around her shoulder and hugged her close.

'It is not going to be this easy', she uttered.

'You are cold, let me get another blanket.'

When he returned from the car, he wrapped Theres and TJ into the warmth, close to his own body. So close, so warm. Gratitude overcame him for this second chance.

'You hurt me...'

'Theres, I know, and I am so sorry. You don't know what I have been through knowing I hurt you!'

'What you have been through? Gosh, I never realized you were this selfish!'

Tom shrank. Theres had not softened towards him as he had believed. It was not only her skin that was cold. He was drowning.

'Think for one moment what you have done to me. You left me, all alone, in Istanbul. After all the promises you have made!'

'Theres, please...'

'No, it is my turn now. You had your go, now listen to me!'

She sat up straight. Cold descended even further.

'The moment you walked away, my life ended! I packed and left the hotel, flew back to Aberdeen on the next available plane. At first, there were tears. The more I thought about it, the angrier I got. How could you do this to me? How could you just dump me without second thoughts after all the promises you made, after all the things we have done together?

'Once back in Aberdeen, I evaluated my options. For a time, I even went back with Ben, just so I wasn't alone. I cancelled Detroit, secured a transfer to Texas instead. Ben came with me, but when he found out about the baby, he left. Even if he hadn't, I would have told him to go. I was all alone when I gave birth. Can you imagine how hard that was?'

Theres stopped to breathe. His arm still sheltered her, even though her onslaught had unsettled him. Tom accepted her reproach, her anger, now that it finally came.

'And then, when I came out of hospital, there I was. New baby, no clue what to do. And all alone! I had to get back to work; there was nobody to look after us. I hated you then. How could you have left me the way you did? But you know, after a while, it got better. TJ is such a happy baby. He was no struggle at all. And I found myself with loads of friends to support me.'

'Theres, please...'

'No. Still my turn. After a while, I even dated. But TJ is al I really care for. He is my son, mine alone. I will be there for him, always. Not like you.'

'That is unfair and you know it!'

'Do I? What is unfair was and still is the way you destroyed what we had, without considering the consequences. That is what is unfair!'

'I can't change the past, but I can be there with you to change the future ... if you only let me!'

She shook her head.

'I told you, I do not need you. TJ does not need you. We have our own life, and it is a good life. It is a life without you and your complications. Tom, no matter what I ever felt for you, I do not want you any longer. You chose. You had your chance.'

She moved away from him.

'You are too late...'

'Please, don't say that ... You are cold, let me get another blanket.'

'No', she said. 'It is time to go. I will take you back and then you can return home tomorrow or whenever suitable. I don't wish to see you again. I have nothing more to say to you'

For now, there were no more words between them. Their positions were clear. Theres might still have feelings for him, but she was too hurt to hear his plea with her heart. She needed time. He would give her that. He had plenty. They would talk again, and he would show her how much he still loved her, and that there was a future for them. He would fight with all he had and he would make it work. This time. He had to. He could not accept losing her yet again. He would find a way to make her see. Tomorrow.

They drove back in silence. Just before her village, Tom thought he saw the first signs of dawn over the horizon.

www.ingramcontent.com/pod-product-compliance
Ingram Content Group UK Ltd.
Pitfield, Milton Keynes, MK11 3LW, UK
UKHW041846190726
13854UKWH00002B/751